Swallowing The Lump

Swallowing The Lump

A Novel

Bridgett Artis

Bridgett Artis
P.O. Box 20056
Tuscaloosa, AL 35402

Library of Congress Cataloging-in Publication Data

Bridgett Artis

Swallowing the Lump/Bridgett Artis-1st ed.

p. cm.

ISBN - 13:978-0-615-23606-3

1. African American Women-Fiction 2. Rap Musicians-Fiction
3. Parole Officer-Fiction 5. Yazell Alabama-Fiction
6. Clients-Fiction 7. University of Ala-Fiction

*First and foremost, I would like to thank my lord and savior
Jesus Christ for choosing me to write this book.*

*To my mom, Rachel Artis for being the loving and
wonderful mother that you are.
For my wonderful son, Rasheed Artis.*

*My sister, Tawanda and my brothers Kevin and Bobby, y'all
are the best.*

*For my aunt Shelia, my uncles Jerry & Larry, and the
entire family, love y'all much.*

To all my fans, enjoy and best wishes.

PROLOGUE

January 2006

Last night was the liveliest and wildest New Year's party I have ever been to," I say as I awake and slide into Henry arms. It seems like a dream come true. I have finally met the man of my dreams. Uncomplainingly, it has been a long wait, but now the wait is finally over. My life is at a new beginning. I know that Henry is the man for me without a second doubt, because looking into his big eyes with the reflection of me every morning makes my day.

"Did you enjoy the party?" I ask Henry joyfully.

"Yeah, it was straight," Henry says as he rolls on top of me and juices me with a sloppy kiss.

"All right, you no what my kissing always lead to, so don't start anything you can't finish," I say teasingly.

Henry leans forward, and kisses me with another sloppy, but more breath taking than normal juicy kiss.

"Where are you going? Don't turn you head," he says gripping my tongue with his lips.

"I need air. I can't breeeathe," I say squealing my words

out as he sucks my tongue, and inhaling my breath softly, but with a firm grip.

Finally, Henry let my tongue go, and rises up off of me. I lay quietly for a second to catch my breath. Out of the blue, I pinch Henry, and say, "You were sucking the air out of me."

Henry grins unpretentiously, and sits at the edge of the bed. "I need to go holler at my people before they leave going back to D.C.," he leans back on one arm, and say.

Henry cousins, Ricky and Teddy came home to visit their Mom two days before Christmas. Ricky and Teddy collaborated six years ago, and open their own detail shop in Washington D.C. This seems to be keeping them out of trouble, and on a more positive path. I once over-heard Henry sister, Beatrice tell their Mom of how happy she is to know that her sons are staying out of trouble with the law, because the bailing them out of jail for disorderly conduct was more of a burden than she could handle.

"I'll be back soon," he says. I look at him sadly hoping to win him over so he will stay.

"I promise, I'll be back soon," he says as he kisses me on my cheek and smile looking warmly into my eyes before closing the door behind him.

The moment after the door closes I instantly crash on the sofa. I'm bombed, and need my second deep sleep. With my second sleep, it seems as if I get the old, and the new sleep that I didn't realize that I needed. After being asleep half of the day, I didn't realize evening had came so soon until my phone ring.

"Hello," I answer lightly.

"Hey baby, what are you doing?" Henry asks optimistically.

"Sleeping," I say as I sit up on the sofa.

"Tired huh," he says a pauses. "Yeah," I say rubbing my fingers through my hair.

"I'm a little beat myself," he says and pauses. "Unpredictably, I'm going to be a little late coming in. Me and the boys are still chilling," he says.

"Hurry, I miss you," I say as I rub my inner thighs after feeling the pain from last night.

Lying on my back should have been the choice I made, but handling my position on top always keeps something on his mind. All I want is a hot salt bath to relax my mind, and my aching muscles to get me on the right track.

"Bang…Bang…Bang…!" I hear a loud knock at my door.

"Shit," I say out loud, and sit up straight. *Who in the hell is this knocking at my door,* I thought.

I quickly put on my house coat, and peeps out of my bedroom window. I can't see a thing, so I tip toe to my front door to listen, but I hear nothing.

CHAPTER 1

Spring 2006

I just got off work, and I'm feeling the wind as it blows freely against my face as I drive with my suede, 2005, red, Mustang, drop top, let back. I'm hungry, and doing 70 miles per hour on the highway when the speed limit is zone at 65 miles per hour on the highway. At the same time, I'm just praying that I don't get stop by the police. In my town, here in Yazell, Alabama, they will give you a ticket for the least little thing you do. My town is small, and consists of a population of 4,000 people, traffic lights, and convenient stores. A great percentage of the people go to the next state that is the closest which is Meridian, Mississippi, to shop, and to handle other special needs that Yazell doesn't offer. The people here are always happy, and friendly. However, the law is strict, and seems unfair to many especially to the ones who do what they call a minor crime, like getting arrested for public intoxication, and feel that they are everyday people, and deserve a second chance without going to jail. Today, if I'm stop by the police for speeding, and yes, I know better, but got to do better, my excuse is, my stomach hurt, and I need to get to a rest room. If that doesn't work, and the officer issue me a ticket, I'll just join it to my speeding ticket list, and pay it off early so that I don't have to go to court, and pay the extra expenses. From working nine hours straight I'm feeling light headed, and dizzy. I haven't eaten since 6:00 a.m. God knows it's time for me to eat. Two more miles down the highway, I'll just stop at my favorite restaurant, and order something to go.

I use to waitress and cook at the Travel and Dine Restaurant until we got a new manager name Earnest. Earnest was one of those managers you hated to see coming. If it was my week to waitress, I had to walk around all day whether I was weary or sick with a smile on my face. The tips were good, but putting up with so many different people and their attitude was draining me mentally. As I change over from my week of being a waitress to being a cook, Earnest wanted us, the cooks, to not take a lunch break, but to courteously smile the eight hours while we cook in the hot ass kitchen. He even had the nerve to put cameras in the kitchen to make sure we don't eat or steal, for whoever in the hell was stealing his food anyway. Now, don't get me wrong, I enjoyed my job. My Co-Workers and I worked well with one another. I guess we knew that we all were in the same boat, trying not to sink. A lot of things changed quickly when Earnest became the manager, the food, the prices, and even our hours were cut from making forty hours a week to twenty-four hours a week. Earnest struggled to keep the business open the five years he was there, because so many cooks walked out, and some got fired for speaking their own mind. I was in the bunch who spoken their own mind.

I realized soon afterwards with the help of my Mama, it was something more for me in life. Shortly after I got fired I went to Claire's Beauty School, and got accepted the following week. Hair is something I always liked to do, but put aside for other things.

Mama had a part time job cleaning for Mr. Lard after his wife had died of cancer. Mr. Lard was an old rich white man. He gave us furniture that was old to him, and he even gave us our first 1974, black, and gold, Station Wagon. Mr. Lard died a year later after his wife passed from a massive heart attack. To me at the age of seven years old, and years afterwards, I thought we were the poorest kids around. We burned fire wood, and had to borrow water from the elderly neighbor that stayed next door to us. At night when the fire goes out it can really get cold. Being curious to learn different things I taught myself how to blow circles in the cold air while everyone else was sleeping. I knew that if I could blow circles in my bed in the middle of the night that ice will be on the ground the next morning. I loved my neighbor for pretending not to know, or for just not knowing at all that we borrowed their water. Mama said we were just borrowing for the time been. I thought we were stealing, because we had to be quiet, and work really fast. Mama never been the type to ask anybody for nothing, she made ends meet the best she knew how. I love my Mama for taking care of us. Although, there was always a million of questions that circulated in my little mind, but I never plan to ask Mama not a one. To me the kids that had nice houses, cars, and cable television were rich. But for some strange reason, they always asked us for a can of polish meat, a bag of chips or a mayonnaise sandwich. Those were a part of our snack until dinner was ready. We never went hungry, not a day. We were happy or at least I was, to have our friends on our porch, and when we ate they ate. One friend name, Crystal, I grew to like after I went to her house, and saw her borrowing water from their neighbor just like us. I smile as I join in to help her. Crystal borrowed water a little different than we did though. She had big buckets to carry. I was weak, and little, so I just carry two jugs. My friend Mark and Bill even helped us go into the woods, and cut down small trees, and pine stumps for fire wood.

Sometimes, when Christmas came, and school started, I wondered where my father was. I heard about him through other people that knew him, and how good he lived, but he never came to visit me. Neither one of us had the same father, so when the thought of being lonely for a father came across our mind, we never talked about it. Hell, I don't know if it came up in anybody else mind, except mine. Wherever I went, especially if I left my Mama side, and went on another isle in the grocery store, the grown folk that knew me, and my Mama would say, "You look just like your daddy." I'll stare them up and down, and wonder, *Who is this lady standing in front of me and telling me that I look like my daddy.*

One hot summer day, Mama was raking the yard to burn leaves. I was in the house looking in the hand mirror, and saying to myself, *I look like my Mama, and I wonder why everybody else is always telling me I look like this man that I don't even know.* I quickly put the mirror down after hearing Mama call my name. I ran outside with no hesitation, because the way Mama was calling my name I knew it meant that it was time to work. As I helped Mama rake the yard the question about my daddy was at the tip of my tongue until I blurted it out.

"Mama, what is my daddy name?" I ask ten minutes after helping Mama.

"I'm yo Daddy," Mama said very impish, and paused. "Clifford Turner says he is yo Daddy," Mama said smiling, and kicking the dust off her feet.

Now who in the world is Clifford Turner, I thought to myself and wanting to ask out loud as I smile back at Mama looking her in the eyes as I pick the leaves up a little bit at a time.

Before Christmas, school, and the people actually put the thought on my mind about my daddy, I was absent minded, and didn't care who my daddy was. Contented, I didn't know, or love either man. All I knew is my Mama, and as long as I have her love, it coverers the empty hole.

Swallowing the Lump

★★★★★★★

Being seven years old a lot of curious thoughts began to explore in my mind. I remember when my brother Kendrick was three; I played Barbershop with him being the client. Mama use to take us to Mr. Bens Barbershop with her as she got serviced with a hair line, and her eyebrows arch. Mama knew how to press, and curl her own hair so there was no need for getting her hair fixed. My brother Kendrick was scared of the Barbershop, he always cried when Mr. Ben waved the clippers at him and said, "You next lil man." Kendrick knew his day was coming, and dreaded that day, so he sat, and cried every time Mama was serviced. I loved following Mama to Mr. Ben Barbershop, and hated when Kendrick cried, because I didn't want to go over my grandma house if he continue to cry. My grandma Mae Bell was mean. Me and my brother always had to take a nap, even if we weren't sleepy. I didn't want to take a nap, so I got a whipping every time, until, I learned to close my eyes, and pretend. Pretending became a big part of my life, and got me in more trouble than I could handle. One Saturday morning, Mama was still asleep. Me and my brother was up, and sitting in the living room watching cartoons. I got Mama big scissors with the orange handle out of the kitchen cabinet. Mama used the scissors to cut our long pants leg after we had worn and torn a hole in the bottom of them.

"Come on," I tell my brother persuasively. "Come play the Barbershop game," I say softly.

He looked at me, and began to whine.

20

"I want cut your hair for real. I'll pretend like I'm cutting it," I say softly and kissed him on his cheek.

I was happy to learn how to trick my Grandmamma, and now I'll trick my brother.

I sat my brother in my lap, and start cutting his hair. He tried to look back, and get out of my lap, but I would say real softly, "Be still boo, I'ma give you some apple juice." I knew apple juice was his favorite juice so I got up, and fix him a cup full.

I turned his head around, and continue to cutting his hair. His hair had bald spots everywhere, but it was so pretty to me. I put him on my hip, and went into Mama bedroom, and woke her up.

"Ma, look at what I did," I said and shaking her arm with a big smile on my face.

Mama opens one eye to look, that one eye got so wide until she had to open the other eye. I knew Mama was going to be happy.

"I know yo ass didn't cut that baby hair!" she said looking like a mad women.

She got up, and got him out of my arms. I watch her ever move as she sat Kendrick on her bed, and open her closet. Mama got her leather belt that was hanging on her favorite jeans, and whipped the snot out of me. Snot was running everywhere. That was my first hurtful whipping that I remembered. Even though, the whipping hurt, and I didn't touch another pair of scissors until later in life, I was happy, because we had a reason to go to the Mr. Ben Barbershop.

Swallowing the Lump

My grandma Mae Bell started to stare at me as I got older, as if she had raised me before, and knew everything I was thinking. One hot August Friday, I'll never forget, Mamas' baby brother, Dennis was home from the military. He was station in Memphis Tennessee. Uncle Dennis took Mama and Kendrick back to Tennessee with him for the weekend. Unknowing, I had to go to school that Friday. The secretary, Mrs. Robinson, came into my 3rd grade class, and gave my teacher a note. My teacher, Mrs. Dubose, read the note before she gave it to me.

"You are to ride the school bus over to your grandma Mae Bell house after school," Mrs. Dubose explains perfectly.

I listen to her, and crumbled the note up, and put it in my pocket after she gave it to me.

The school bell ring. My cousin Bee-Bee, who stayed down the street from our Grandma, was waiting by my room door. He had left his fifth grade hall, and was on my hall soon after the first bell had rung for all bus riders.

"Granny said for me to put you on the right bus, because yo Mama and brother is gone to Tennessee with yo uncle Dennis. They left you," he giggled.

"Bee-Bee knows he can't fight. I always had to take up for him, and he knows that I get mad just because, and will fight to feel better, so he betta leave me alone. *I ought to beat him up now, but I want my mama,* I thought. I knew the secretary, the teacher, and my cousin were all lying to me. *My Mama wouldn't have left me. She loves me, so why would she leave, and not take me with her,"* I thought. So, I fix them for lying to me, and got on the bus to go home.

"Hey, Mr. Pete," I speak to the bus driver.

"You are the only one riding today?" Mr. Pete asks before he closes the bus door.

"Yes sir," I say and walk to the last seat on the bus.

I place my book bag on the seat, and let the window down.

"You gonna get it," My cousin Bee-Bee yelled standing outside the bus looking at me angrily.

I laughed at him, and put my index finger under my right eye, and held it down with my tongue sticking out. I sat on my book bag, and enjoyed my ride home better than any ride I had ever taken. I was so excited because ain't nothing like going home after school, and seeing my Mama.

I stomped down the bus steps loudly, and ran speedily through the path that was behind my house. I tried to open the front screen door, but it was locked. I ran back to the back door, and it was locked.

"Mama, open the door," I bang on the door and yelled.

Mama didn't answer. I sat in the corner of the other front door that didn't have a screen with my head folded on my knee. I was mad, and wanted to know why Mama wouldn't open the door.

An hour later I looked up, and saw my grandma, Mae Bell, and Bee-Bee. They had walked in the hot summer heat all the way across town to get me. Across town is really far when walking. I had never seen my Grandma as mad as she was looking with sweat running down her face. My heart started beating a triple beat.

"I-I-I-I...gonna, beat yo lil bad ass!" Grandma said stammering.

Grandma stammered a lot when she was mad. I jumped off the porch, and ran behind a big pine tree that sat in the front of the yard. She grabbed me by my left arm, and told Bee-Bee to break her two switches off a bush, and wrap them together. I tried to pull away, but she held me so tight until I just sat in the middle of the road. Grandma raised her arm high in the air.

"I knew it, I knew it! I knew you was going to do it yo way. Yo way ain't right," she preached and made me walk in front of her all the way to her house as she pop me with those two switches over and over again.

Grandma Mae Bell was right I always had to do it my way. I was hurt from the whipping, but I was mostly hurt, because Mama had left me.

Grandma Mae Bell had a reputation of getting what she wanted or raising hell, until she got it. Nobody messed with my Grandma Mae Bell.

I remember Grandma Mae Bell had this path between two empty houses that she walked through to go over to the bootleg house, and buy her a bottle of moonshine. There was a middle age couple that moved in one of the houses from Chicago. They didn't want anybody else to trespass through their yard so they put up a, No Trespassing Sign. Grandma continued on to walk through the path over to Mr. Bulk house to buy her a gallon of moonshine. Mr. Bulk loved to sell moonshine, dip snuff, and listen to his roc-cola all day, and half of the night. Grandma dragged me tightly by my hand after she had gotten her moonshine back through the path. I was shoeless, and the rocks were hot to my feet.

The new neighbors were a mix couple. Mrs. Patterson is white, and Mr. Patterson is black. Mr. Patterson is from Yazell. His Mama left him the house, and he wanted to move from the north back to the south to live in his house.

Just as me and my Grandma got to the middle of the path, Mrs. Patterson stood in her door, and yelled to my grandma, "Did you read the sign? It reads, No Trespassing," she said and then put her hands on her hip.

"Hell nah, I didn't see no sign!" Grandma Mae Bell yelled.

I didn't think my Grandma could even read, because I knew I couldn't, I was still determine to get out of the Blue Tail Horse book, so I could graduate to the next book.

"Who in the hell do you think you talking to bitch?" My grandma said as she stopped and stood in the path and let my hand go.

"I'm talking to you," she said.

"I'll beat yo ass if you come off that porch," my grandma yelled.

"I'm going to call the police on you if you walk back through my yard," she said going back inside and locking her screen door behind her.

"You and the police can kiss my ass. Call the police!" My grandma yelled and picked up a stick that was lying in the path.

Swallowing the Lump

I knew my grandma had been drinking, and would have hit Mrs. Patterson across the head if she had stepped off her porch. I wanted to see my grandma hit Mrs. Patterson, because even being little I was mad, and had a rock in my hands. Grandma grabbed me by my hand raging mad, and pulled me through the path back to her house.

It didn't take Mrs. Patterson long to accept the path as being the path that everybody in the neighborhood walked through. She had to deal with it or get ran from the neighborhood.

Later on that evening after Grandma had given me a whipping I sat across the dinner table, and watch her as she cut her collard greens into small pieces.

"You remind me so much of yo Mama. You stop thinking those bad ways right now," Grandma said talking fast.

I sat quietly, and didn't say a word.

"Lord, they say that everything you do will come back, and now, I'm getting it double. Lord, I pray that you guide my Grandbaby."

I didn't understand a word my Grandma was saying, but I look at her in her eyes, and she looked me back in mine.

Grandma Mae Bell died of natural causes. I was too little to understand my Grandma, and why she raised so much hell. Now as I think about Grandma Mae Bell, I love, and miss her much.

CHAPTER 2

The Travel and Dine Restaurant has expanded a lot over the years since it's been under new management. Every five years it's goes under new management. A service station was added on the side of the restaurant for regular customer and traveling guest to get gas, and shop for snacks.

"What's up Q-man? I see y'all have these machines on a roll today. Has anybody hit jackpot yet?" I ask.

"What's up? What's up baby? Nobody have hit all day. The machine is waiting on you, and is going to hit any minute," he says grinning from ear to ear.

"Yeah, right, I'll try my luck after I order my food," I say passing his cash registered and entering the restaurant.

A tall lady hostess name Samantha greets me with a

smile, and a menu. Since I know what I want, and my mind is focusing on what Q-Man just said, I just order, and pay for my food, and heads straight for the gambling machine.

Q-man is an Arab. He and his family are taking over all the new and local gas stores around here. I stop in for gas, something quick to eat, and sometimes to gamble on the machines so he knows my face by hard. Q-Man is cool people or at least he pretend to be cool to keep the business flowing. Nevertheless, they are all about that money, and stay open all night 24/7.

"I told you, you will hit jackpot today," he says scribbling his words out so fast until I can hardly understand him.

"Jackpot, you call thirty-dollars a jackpot. Y'all have those machines rigged up so you can't win anything. They are to just tease the customers with a little money to keep them playing, and coming back," I say at the register and handing him my ticket.

"You know I won't do that, the machines hit all the time," he grins and says as he reads my ticket.

"I'm going to use the ticket for gas," I say.

"Pump seven is on for you," he says.

"Are you Linda?" A young waitress asks dressed in black jeans and a white button shirt with a white pin on her upper left pocket written in red letters that reads, *Hello my name is Jessie.*

She is a cute girl around the age of 21, but her hair is screaming, "Please help me!"

"Yes, I'm Linda," I say as I leave the store registered and

walk towards her.

"Your order is ready," she says, and gives me my food in a large white to go tray.

"Thank you," I say with a smile and give her a two dollar tip with my business card.

I open my plate of hot wings, and fries to make sure that everything is just as I ordered. You know with new management, things can change within a blink of an eye. Quite naturally, Mrs. O'theia always hooks me up. She's been working at the Travel and Dine Restaurant for fourteen years, and has seen many people come and go. Despite the fact that she has had back surgery, and haven't been able to work many hours she still enjoy the few hours that she has. Her oldest son, Brandon, wants her to stop working, and move to San Francisco, California, with him. Mrs. O'theia loves her home, and is sixty-four years old, and is set in her own ways. She loves her son Brandon, but with him being a homosexual, secretly hurts her to her heart, so she rather stay home, and deal with it far away.

"Excuse me Linda," A soft voice yells at me as I open the store door to leave.

"Do you accept walk-ins?" The waitress asks.

"Yes, if I'm not to busy. Calling for an appointment is better. I can get you in, and out much quicker without you having to wait." I say surely and pause. "What's your name?" I ask to make sure I pronounce it correctly.

"Jessie Smith," she says and continues to read my business card.

"Just call me," I say and begin pumping my gas.

Swallowing the Lump

This has got to be the slowest pump I've ever used. Twenty-nine, thirty, it's about time, I say to myself and hang the gas nozzle up.

I adjust my seat, and fasten my seat belt. I'm so hungry, and I know I need to wait until I get home to eat, but my stomach is calling for my food now.

As I put my tray in my lap, and bites my first wing, I couldn't help, but to notice, a tall, two-hundred, and twenty pound, black man walking. His black, Timberland boots a size twelve or fourteen makes me say, "Damn," and choke slightly off my wings. His black, Timberlands jean, black jacket with no sleeves, accompany by a long sleeve, white union shirt underneath just tops his style off temptingly.

Who is this sexy ass brother, walking across the front of my car? I clear my throat and ask myself as I take another bite into my hot wings with nothing to chase the burning sensation down.

I have to find out, I say to myself as I curve my neck to the side and perk my lips.

I hurried up, and open my car door, and start to brush my size nine, Baby Phat Jeans off pretending as if I had drop something in my lap.

"Excuse me. Do I know you from somewhere?" I asked after I saw him looking and continuing to stare at me.

"Henry, Henry Bash," I stand up straight and say with a surprise look on my face. "Is that you?" I ask.

"Yes that's me, and who are you?" he asks as he fumbles with a Cigar.

"I'm Linda Lax. I remember you from high school," I say and offer him a hand shake.

Bridgett Artis

Whenever County High had a football game, Henry Bash was there. Most games, he was not allowed to enter, unless he sneaked himself in through the back fence that was surrounded by bushes.

I remember County High vs. Taylor High School. It was the last game for the school season. Both schools were rivalry schools when it came to sports. County High had won the game, and ended their season with victory. Henry was standing outside the Taylor High School Bus meddling, and daring the football team to get off their bus.

"I bet yo punk ass want get off that bus!" Henry yelled to a team member from Taylor High.

Taylor High football team and fans was already extremely upset after losing the game. One of the team members yelled out the bus window, and said, "Ain't no punks on this bus."

He opened the back exit door of the bus, and he and the rest of the team fled off. The coaches and parents all got out of the way; because all hell was broken loose. Henry had caused the worst disaster. Taylor High and County High football team plus the fans from both teams collided.

Remembering Henry from that school fight is the first thing that comes to my mind after seeing him again.

"What year did you finish?" He asks and stretches his head.

"I finish in ninety-four," I say as I chew my hot wing real slow so he wouldn't be able to tell that my mouth is burning the shit out of me.

"It's nice to see you again," I say and sit back into my car.

Swallowing the Lump

"Good to see you too," he says as he continues to fumble with his cigar.

"Damn, he is cute, and sexy," I say to myself as I look back at him through my rearview mirror.

★★★★★★

Driving, and eating is so messy, and I don't have any napkins in my car. My stern wheel is all greasy, and my mouth is on fire. Coming up to the next traffic light is a Parade Gas Store. I drive my red, Mustang between a black, Nissan Altima, and a green Grand Prix, and go inside.

There is nothing I like better than a cold mellow-yellow with ice to quench my thirst, I thought and drink with satisfaction.

Before I completely get in the car, I wipe the grease from the hot wings off my stern wheel with a napkin that I receive from the cashier.

"What's up girl?" My friend Melody Hyper speaks as she pulls to the gas pump in her gray, Mitsubishi Mirage.

Melody is a sweet lady with a good heart, but sometimes I wonder about her. She is full figured, and her skin is so yellow, she looks very pale up close. She has long black silky hair that falls to her back that she keeps in a pony-tail.

Melody is much older than I. Our friendship started after I finished high school. I met her through my baby father, Patrick. Patrick aunt, Teresa and Melody were best friends until Teresa job offered her a higher salary, and a new position for her to relocate, and move to Kentucky.

34

I can remember like it was yesterday on how our friendship all begin.

"Hey I'ma tell you something," Melody said the first time I saw her over to Teresa house.

Teresa was having a barbeque. Melody and I was the only one in the kitchen fixing us a plate. Patrick and I had been having our ups and down in our relationship. Melody knew the entire scoop about everything. Patrick couldn't keep his business to himself. He had to tell his aunt, and she told Melody.

"If you want to be with Patrick for a long time, I'll help you," Melody said.

By Melody volunteering to help me caught me by surprise. I was new to the relationship life, and was desperate for any advice even if it meant taking advice from a stranger.

Patrick and I started dating in high school. We always hook up after school over Teresa house every chance we got even if we lied, and told our parents that we had to practice late. Early in our relationship I became pregnant, and had a son, name Flip. Patrick was the number one quarter back at County High School, and I was the state champ in the 200 meter, Track and Field. Patrick and I dated until our son was four years old. We grew apart, and went our separate ways. A couple years after the break up, Patrick was in a terrible accident. The accident caused him to be paralyzed from the waist down. His mother wasn't able to give him the proper care he needed so she had no choice, but to place him in the Nursing Home for therapy, and proper care. Flip and I visit a lot along with Patrick other female friends that are hoping one day the therapy will help, and he'll be able to walk again. But, before I threw the towel in on our relationship, I was willing to do, and listen to anything.

Melody lived on a street called the block. Every dude in town hung on the block. They barbecued on the block, hooked up with their other females, shot dice you name it, it was there. Melody told me everything she thought she knew. If Patrick was on the block talking to another female she called, and even if Rodney was on the block cheating right before her very own eyes she called me. I found myself tagging along, and listening to Melody until I started using my own head. Melody was five years older than I, and she loved guys that were in their early twenties. With me being the age of twenty-two at the time, I looked up to her, and was desperate for the information on how to keep my man.

It was February 13, 1996, the night before Valentines Day. I receive a phone call from Melody at 7:00 p.m.

"Yeah girl, it's going down tonight on Fifteenth-Street. It suppose to be a secret, but I heard Patrick telling Rodney to tell all of his friends about the party he's having tonight, and to bring lots of dollars, because strippers are performing," she said.

Rodney is Melody on, and off again lover. He's twenty-one years old, and is short with long dreads that hang to the middle of his back. Melody and Erica, takes good care of him. Melody works part-time at the Best Choice Cleaners. Erica is the mother to their two kids. Latoya is three years old, and

Willie is one years old. Rodney doesn't have a job, and feel that since he baby sit occasionally while Erica is at work that that's fully taking care of the kids. Erica is a Registered Nurse at St. Mayes, Veterans Hospital, in Hopper Mississippi. Erica works twelve hours for five nights a week plus an extra hour with the drive to work. I was puzzled, and wonder why Melody wanted to share somebody else man, so I ask her. She told me that he loves her, and is just there with Erica for the kids. I was young, and of course it sounded true, so I believed it. Melody knew Erica, but Erica didn't know at the time that Melody exists.

"Why are you telling me this?" I asked very hesitantly.

"I told you that I am going to help you. If you don't keep up with Patrick somebody else will. We have to go, and see what's going on. Nobody will ever know we are there. I'll drive my uncle truck, and park it over by the Brown Creek Park on Sixteenth Street, and we'll walk from there," Melody said.

I held the phone quietly in shock, because no one had ever called me with news about Patrick.

"Girl, I don't know about doing that. Want we be stalking them," I said and pause.

"You call it what you want to call it, but every women that has a secure relationship has stalk their man, or gathered information one way or another.

To me stalking is a form of insanity. I already had enough on my plate from learning how to pretend, and learning how to stalk is something that I don't know if I'm ready for or want to do. But as I pause for a minute, and think about it, *I need all the information I can get, and once things boiled down, and I put two and two together, I'm going to be to tuff to handle in my own little way.*

"We want be long. We're just gonna be there long enough to see what's going on, and leave," she say stridently. "I'm gonna bringing my blade just in case though," she mumbled.

"What you say," I asked.

"Nothing, but I promise. I promise we want be long, she said loudly. "I can be over in ten minutes to pick you up," Melody said convincingly.

"Ok," I said, and hung up the phone.

CHAPTER 3

I walked back, and forth in my apartment wonder ing, *What in the hell was I getting myself into.* Stalking is something I never did or had a reason to do, but Melody made it seem like it was all a part in a relationship. Therefore, I was ready physically, and felt like I was fixing to go, and play cops, and robbers. That's the game me, and my friends use to play on our 12 speed bicycle. I remember riding it in all gears, and never getting caught. I peeped out of my window as soon as I heard the loud, white truck reached the corner of my apartment complex. I quickly put on my blue and white converse tennis, my black hood sweater, blue jeans, and dashed out the door.

"Hey," I speak as I sat inside the truck.

Melody was dressed in all black from her black hood

sweater to her black leather boots. After I sat in the truck Melody impression gave me the feeling like we was going to do more than just stalk, and leave.

"What's up? Where's your baby?" Melody asked.

I hope she didn't think that I would bring Flip along with me this time of that night, especially to stalk his dad, I thought.

"My Mama is helping me a lot more since I'm in beauty school. He is living with her until I finish school," I said looking at her nervously.

"We gonna catch these sap-suckers tonight," She said, and snapped her finger, and rolled her neck.

Melody was glorified, and laid back with doing this. To her it was just another trip to the gas store. I was down with the stalking, but worried at the same time. I didn't know or trust Melody well enough with having my back incase shit don't go as plan.

"Give me the keys," I requested after she took the keys out of the switch. I was thinking Melody might try something more risky than the stalking.

"Damn, don't be scared. Here, get the keys," she muttered spreading her nose open and bucking her tiny eyes as she gave me the keys.

I didn't give a damn about Melody cursing, and handing me the keys the way she did. All I cared about was seeing what we needed to see, and getting the hell out of sight, smoothly.

"Which house is it?" I asked as we tip behind an abandon houses.

"That blue up stairs house across the street where you

see all the cars parked. We need to get a little closer so we can get a good look," Melody said and tips behind two bushes that sit in front of the old house.

"Our ass is gonna get caught if we get any closer. Patrick always watches his back no matter what he's doing," I whisper cautiously.

Melody look back at me, and shook her head, and kept on moving closer.

This nut is going to get caught, and if she does get caught for being hard headed, I'm going to take off, and leave her crazy ass, I thought seriously to myself.

"There goes Patrick outside on the phone," she whispered, and got down on her knees. "Look, I see twelve girls going inside. Each one of them has on a long black coat. I bet that they're naked," she said.

"What in the hell is going on," I said as I eased beside Melody to get a good look for myself.

Seeing Patrick standing on the porch of the house with girls walking in to shake their ass had me in a state of shock. I really didn't know what to think or do. I was ready to go home, and think to myself.

"Girl, my cell phone is vibrating," I said.

I look nervously to see who was calling.

"It's Patrick, and he going to keep calling me if I don't answer," I said to Melody as I pulled her shoulder and show her the phone.

"Don't answer it," Melody yelled in a whispering voice.

"I'll tell him, I was taking a shower, and didn't hear the

43

phone," I said.

"I want tell his ass nothing. Look at what he's doing. Girl you betta wake up, and see what you see," she said and rolled her eyes.

Standing out there with Melody I was beginning to feel like I wasn't thinking for myself, and was been told what to do by her. I know she is a little older than me, but Melody doesn't know that I hate it when somebody bosses me around, and try to tell me what to do.

"Shit, it's raining, and is cold out here, lets go," I said angrily as I got the keys out of my pocket.

"Hell nah! I see Rodney's black, eighty-eighty, Oldsmobile Cutlass over there with them gold, five star, rims on it back up in the driveway," she said biting her nail. "I'm about to go, and knock on the damn door."

"No the hell you ain't," I said pulling her back by her hood. "This is getting crazy, and is going to get out of control if we don't get out of here," I said.

Melody looked at me as if she was going to have a panic attack.

"Nah, better yet, I'm gonna cut his tires," she said with tears covering her eyeballs.

I knew this shit was going to happen. Melody saw what she wanted to see, but can't handle it, and leave. I don't give a damn right now about what I see, because I know how to pretend, and handle my thoughts in a way that will satisfy me later.

"Girl stop crying, and get yourself together. You can't cut

that dude tires, because you know he is crazy about that car," I said as I put my hood over my head.

"Fuck him, and his car. You act like you is scared. I'm the one fixing to do the cutting.

"Her slow crazy ass is fixing to mess up, and get caught," I mumbled, and rest my hands on top of my head.

"I ain't scared I can't pay for nobody else shit, I don't even own my own ride, and talking about messing up somebody else ride.

"Well, I'm fixing to do it. I'll be right back you just watch out," she said.

"Damn, you are hard headed too," I mumbled and put my hands on my hip.

Melody and I are here together and I can't leave her now, because she may do something crazier than what we are already doing. If she gets caught, or in trouble with the law I may get in trouble for being involve as well, and I ain't going down like that, so I might as well help her flat these tires, smoothly, and quickly, so we can get the hell out of here before things get out of control, I thought. "How many razor blades do you have?" I asked.

"Hell yeah, that's what I'm talking about. I brought two just in case," Melody said with a smile on her face and pulls an extra blade out of her pocket.

Melody brought an extra razor blade just incase, because she had plan before she left her house to do more than just stalk.

"I'll get the two back tires, and you do the front, and we're leaving," I demand.

Swallowing the Lump

Melody followed me as I slid behind the back of a gray, Chevy Suburban that was parked in front of the drive way, and blocking Rodney car. We stayed in a squatting position while we jumped from left to right stabbing each tire.

"I wished I had some sugar so I can put some in his gas tank," Melody said as she stops and looks back at Rodney car tires go down.

"Lets damn go!" I demand as I turn around, and look back at her.

Melody and I was tickled while running fast. When we arrived back to the truck, we lean on the cold wet truck laughing, and holding our stomach.

"Damn," Melody grunts as she turns the switch. I need you to get out, and push the truck. Sometimes it needs a push before it'll start," she said.

"Forget that, I can't push this big ass truck. I'll get in the driver seat, and let you push," I said looking at my cold hands as they tremble.

Melody put the truck in park, and walked behind the truck. I scooted from the passenger seat to the driver seat.

"I got the gear on the N letter so push," I said.

My use to be step dad, Big Papa, use to fix on cars, so I learned a thing or two by watching him. Big Papa name was self explanatory when or wherever you saw him. He was a big tall man, but he act like he was the same age as I. Our station wagon was broken down in our yard, and every time he came over to our house to see Mama, and fix her car, Mama had left, and walked to town. He couldn't keep up with Mama by himself, so he'll tell me and my brother to put on our shoes, and lets go to town. I was glad, and didn't like the neighbors who watched us. I guess I just didn't like anyone who watched us for Mama. Big Papa had nappy dreads that stood on top of his head like a wild fire, and his black comeback-boots made flopping noise every time he walked. When he got too far ahead of us by walking so fast, me and my brother would run in order for us to catch up with him. Every car that came by our house to take Mama to town I remember it, so each time a noticeable car went through the traffic light I was looking for Mama. We stood patiently on the main corner that every car had to drive pass. Some days we found Mama, and some days we didn't. I even had gotten to the point that I'll wait good until she walk to town, and I'll tell my brother lets follow Mama. I always knew where Mama went, the spots she stop at, and the people who knew where she was at. The pool hall was her favorite stop. Mama likes to talk, and see people, so I'll make it my business with my brother tagging along to sit in the pool hall window, and wait for the old man who works in the pool hall to come out.

"What are y'all doing down here?" he asked.

"You saw my Mama?" I asked openly.

"Yeah, she just walked to the barbershop," he said.

That was all I wanted to hear. We walk across the train track headed for the barbershop, and there Mama was, not far from the barbershop, and sitting under a pecan tree on a bucket talking to an old man, and eating pecans. Mama looked like she was delighted to see us. She gave us some pecans, and we

47

sat next to her side.

Mama let us had our way a few times until I got out of hand with it. She couldn't walk anywhere without me later coming behind her. The days that Mama would be sitting on the sofa with her mirror in her lap and making her face up so pretty, I just couldn't take it. I wanted to know why Mama always got so pretty to go to town. I told Kendrick to put on his shoes we're going to go, and find Mama. We walked happily a block up the road, and turn the curve. Mama was sitting at the neighborhood laundry mat waiting on us with two switches wrap together. Mama whipped the hell out of both of us, and threw a rock at our dog. The dog liked to follow her too. It was the neighbor dog, but he stayed at our house like he was our dog. We all ran back home, and never followed Mama ourselves again until Big Papa became our step dad. Though, our dog followed her one day without us, and couldn't keep up after she caught a ride, and we never seen him again since that day. Weeks had gone pass since me and my brother had followed Mama. Suddenly, Big Papa came by our house, and Mama wasn't home. He told me and my brother to find our shoes and lets go find Mama. I spotted Mama riding pretty with another man going through the traffic light.

"There go mama, there go mama!" I said screaming to Big Papa and pointing at the car.

Mama saw us, and got out the car by the grocery store across the street, and we walked over to her. Mama had an expression on her face like, *what the hell is y'all doing down here.* She didn't say a word. Big Papa, Mama, me and my brother all walked back home with smiles on our faces. At least I did.

Big Papa finally fix Mama car. He said that he had to be at his own house more, and he'll come back to see us, but he never came back. Weeks later, I asked Mama where he was, and she said at his own place. That didn't sound right, but the way she said it made me not want to ask another question.

"Thank God it cranked up, because the last thing we need is for someone to stop, and give us a jump off," I said to Melody as she hops back in on the passenger side.

"You betta get back over here, I ain't driving this truck," I said and slide back to the passenger seat as Melody got out and came back to the driver seat.

I just learned how to spy on my man. I didn't know whether I was happy or sad from what I just saw, but I shook the sad feeling off, and began to hear a voice echoing in my ear saying, *you don't need him if you have to spy.* I was in love with Patrick, and I knew that the voice was lying too me.

"Are you alright?" Melody asked.

"I'm fine," I said and sat up straight.

"Just wait, it'll take a while, but you'll learn, because I'm going to help you," Melody said.

Melody called me day and night a year straight with new ideas of how we can keep Rodney and Patrick for ourselves. I learn fast, but the more I learned I became depressed. However, I grew to like Melody, because we had plenty of laughs behind our devilment, but at the same time my depression became severe. I thought I was going nuts. I told Melody how I was feeling, and she said that she has the same feelings, and she gets treated for hers. She advised me to go to her doctor, and to explain to him how I was feeling, and I did. Dr. Madison wrote me a prescription for some pills called Zoloft. I told Melody what her doctor prescribed me and she said that those are the same pill that she takes. One evening after I had gotten off work I took the Zoloft. That shit had me so slow, and special that I couldn't get mad or think fast if I wanted to. *When this shit wears off, a nigger can't pay me to convince myself that I'm depress, and take a Zoloft,* I thought to myself. As soon as I returned to being myself again, we joke about the way the pill made us feel, and boy, we laughed our asses off. I discovered instantly that Zoloft wasn't for me, but Melody said that she needs them. Regardless of my depression, Melody was happy, because she was use to doing what she does, and to her we had won. Winning always makes me happy, but deep inside I was losing, and didn't understand. I wanted to distance myself from her, and be my normal self again, but Melody was like a fly that wouldn't go away.

★★★★★★★

Two years came in a flash and by now Melody and I did any and everything when it came down to Rodney and Patrick. Suddenly, I started to feel like a wild lunatic. Thank God, I finished Beauty School, and realize that I needed to get my life moving on the right track. I couldn't, and didn't know how to enjoy, and love myself for smoothly stalking, and running behind Patrick and Rodney only to satisfy Melody.

50

I remember one morning, I awaken to use the bathroom, and my phone rang.

"Hey girl, it's Melody, I need you to ride somewhere with me," she said in a crackling voice.

"Are you out of your mind? It is two o'clock in the morning, and it is raining badly. I'm not getting out tonight," I said looking in my medicine cabinet for my Pepto-Bismol.

"You gonna miss out," Melody said angrily, and hung up the phone.

Later that morning about four-thirty a.m., I received another phone call from Melody.

"Have you heard what happen?" she asked.

"No I haven't heard," I said and sat up in the middle of my bed rubbing my eyes.

"Patrick and Rodney were in a car accident. Rodney burst his knee wide open, and Patrick can't move from waist down. Girl you need to get to the hospital quick," Melody said frantically.

I quickly put on my clothes, and house shoes, got Flip out of bed, and rushed to the hospital.

Arriving at the hospital I saw cars parked everywhere. I pulled to the front of the hospital looking for a place to park. Patrick mother, Mrs. Hall, spotted me, and ran to the car.

"What happen?" I asked her as she reaches for Flip.

Mrs. Hall is unquestionable crazy about all six of her boys, and Patrick is the youngest.

"Somebody cut the front tier on the Ford Explore that Patrick was driving. He and Rodney were leaving the club.

Patrick was taking Rodney to the Holiday Inn Hotel, and the front tier blew out," Mrs. Hall said worriedly.

"Are they alright?" I asked.

Mrs. Hall just shook her head.

I left Mrs. Hall standing in front of the hospital holding Flip while I quickly got into the car, and found a place to park. Memories of all of the good and bad times we shared rotated in my brain over and over again. Even though the bad experiences mentally out weighed the good, but never did I once wish for Patrick to get hurt.

"Well, what did the doctor say?" I asked.

"The doctor said that Patrick may be temporary paralyze," Mrs. Hall said and wiped her tears with a napkin that the nurse had given her earlier.

She kisses Flip on his cheek, and said that every thing will be alright. Flip was six years old, and didn't understand much what was going on. He cried a little, only, because Mrs. Hall was crying as she talked.

"Rodney knee burst open terribly. He's getting stitches, and will have a limp for the rest of his life." She said.

"Can Flip go see Patrick?" I asked with my hand resting on my forehead.

"Not tonight, he's in I.C.U, and no visitors or children are aloud. I'll pick Flip up as soon as the doctor says he can have visitors," she said and kisses Flip on his cheek before she handed him back to me.

I left walking back to my new, 93 Buick Lasaber that Mama had given me to use for transportation to beauty school, and to take Flip to the doctor. Mama had work hard cleaning houses to buy her a new car, and when she gave it to me to use I knew that I had to take care of it.

My mind was completely blank. I didn't know what to think. The worse was taking over my thoughts. I quickly control my mind, prayed, and thought positive thoughts. As I open my car door I heard foot steps. It was Melody standing soaked, and wet behind my car.

"Why aren't you at the hospital with Rodney?" I asked puzzled.

"Girl, I can't— I mean, I don't want to go inside. Tell me what you heard," she said trembling

"You are the one who called me. I thought you already knew," I said as I put Flip inside the car.

"Did they say what caused the accident?" She asked.

"They had a blow out," I said and shut the back car door.

"Hey," I said, and paused while staring at her. "You didn't have anything to do with this?" I asked.

"Mmm, uh," she muttered.

"Well, did you?" I asked looking her straight in her eyes. I knew something wasn't right.

"Hell no," Melody said, and began to dust off her dirty black jeans. "I need you to give me a ride home. I have been walking all morning, and please don't tell anyone you saw me."

Something wasn't right, but I was in to deep with her to tell, and besides I didn't want to know what she had gotten herself into.

"Thanks girl. I owe you one," Melody said as she got out of the back seat of the car.

★★★★★★

I believe Melody caused the *accident, but I never said another word about the* accident to her or anyone else. I begin to think that she was some type of crazy person. Melody didn't care who she hurt as long as she got her way. Every since Melody told me how her father murder her mom, and then himself right before her own eyes, I always felt sorry for her. Sometimes I wished I had never asked what happen.

"It was a hot summer night. My brother had stayed over to his friend house for a birthday sleep over. Mama told daddy that he had to pack his bags and leave," Melody said as we sat on her door step late one fall night.

"Our relationship is at a dead end, and I'm tired of your lazy no having sex ass. I got a new man now, and he fucks me all night. He's not like yo sorry ass who only last three minutes. So get yo drunk lost job ass out of my house. When I come back from Frankie Mayes party you betta be gone." My Mama fussed.

My Mama had already drunk a six pack of Colt 45 that night, and Daddy was drinking Taka Vodka. I stood behind the door, and continue to peep from my bedroom. Mama left slamming the door behind her. Daddy was very angry. He saw me peeping, and yelled, "Get yo little ass back in the bed."

Bridgett Artis

I was only eight years old. The sound of his voice scared me. I ran, and jump back in the bed, and pull the covers over my head. Hours later I woke up after I heard the front door slam.

"I told you to have yo ass out of my house," Mama screamed at Daddy.

Daddy stood up from his recliner, and grabbed his shot gun that he had sitting behind his recliner. "Yeah, you've been out with Paul over at Frankie Mayes. I already knew that nigga wasn't to be trusted. He worked beside me everyday, and been sleeping with my women all this time," Daddy said as he stood to his feet, and stumbled.

Paul had moved up the street from us, from North Carolina. He love to go over Frankie Mayes on the weekend, and that is where Mama and Paul relationship all started.

Frankie ran a gambling house. She had parties on the weekend, and sold whiskey.

"I told you, you ain't nothing, but a whore! I'll kill you," he said, and raised his shot gun.

"Get out, get the hell out!" Mama screamed to the top of her crackling lungs.

"Bang!" The trigger was pulled.

My hand was over my ears while they argued until I heard the loud noise. I got out the bed, and walk in the living room. I saw Mama lying on the floor. She was covered in blood holding her stomach. I ran, and got on top of her, and screamed, "Daddy stop. Don't hurt Mama!" He pulled me off her, and told me to go back to my room. I ran out the house, and down the street to get my uncle. He lived four houses down. My uncle was already on his way after hearing the gun shot. By the time we gotten to the house Daddy had ran into the woods behind our house. Mama was dead on the floor covered in blood. Five minutes later we heard a gun shot. Daddy had shot, and killed himself in the woods.

CHAPTER 4

Years have passed, and Melody and I still remains friends. I try to keep my distance to move for ward, and not get caught back up in the past, but sometimes I still have that desire, and want to talk or know what is up. It's like an addiction that I don't want to let go. I feel like I may need her in the future.

"Hey, girl," I speak back to Melody and give her a hug.

"What you doing off work so early?" Melody asks.

"Girl, I finish early when Flip has football practice, so I can pick him up on time," I say and pause.

"Hey, do you remember Henry Bash?" I ask.

Melody knows everybody, and if I need information on someone all I have to do is ask her. But, I have to sugar coat the question, because if Melody had the least little idea that

I'm interested, she'll take matters into her own hands. I mean, hook it up top speed.

"The only Henry I know is the one who use to hang with O.D. back in high school?" Melody says with her finger on her right chaw.

O.D. was the school bully who originally started the school fights. I remember when O.D. got into a fight with Terry Dale and broke his neck, and from that day on no one mess with O.D. It was our junior and senior skip day. O.D. was dating Susan Dorsal. He only wanted to be with her on the weekend and not through the weekday. Susan was black as smut, real skinny with big eyes and big breast. She was very smart and in all honor classes. She did all of O.D. school assignments for him. That day we all met at the park, and most of us were a couple, and only a few were single. Susan sat alone on the swing set, whereas O.D. was flirting with the new chick name Carmen Banks from Mississippi.

Terry Dale was cute, short, and sexy. He played the saxophone in the band. He could hold his saxophone and rock from side to side in a slow motion. All the girls stopped what they were doing and focus all their attention on him. I always eyeballed his hips in every direction that they move during the school football games. Terry was a single senior and knew how to make anybody laugh. As Susan sat alone on the swings staring at the dirt, the rest of us were all hugged up kissing and barbecuing. We weren't paying much attention to the single ones. Terry walked over to Susan and began to push her on the swings. Their conversation and laughter caught everybody attention, especially O.D. O.D. left Carmen standing against his car and walked over to the swings.

"What's the fuck you doing talking to my girl?" O.D. asked.

"How is she your girl and you were over their talking to another chick?" Terry argued.

Susan jumped up from the swings and stood closely by Terry side. O.D. didn't argue back with Terry. He pushed the back of Terry head with all his strength to the iron pole of the swing. Terry almost fell, but he caught his grip and swung and jabbed O.D. in his nose. O.D. didn't take any mercy for Terry after the jab, because he body-slams Terry awfully. He jumped on top of Terry and beat his head over and over again until we heard a popping sound. Patrick and the rest of the boys quickly pulled O.D. off of Terry.

I walked over to my classmate Carla and told her, "Lets go before the police and ambulance come."

I was suppose to be at school and wasn't any way I was going to get caught at the park. Carla was always cool and down for whatever so we left everybody and went over to her house and waited until 3:00 p.m. Carla mom was very strict on her. All Carla could do was go to school and back home. But little did her mom know she was the wildest of us all, especially when it came to skipping school and stealing her mama car late at night while she was asleep. Carla mom work from nine to five, which gave me enough time to chill and be gone.

The next day in school everybody was upset and felt

sorry for Terry. Terry later recovered, but wasn't the same. He couldn't play his saxophone nor march in the band any more.

"I guess. I just saw him at the Travel and Dine Restaurant, and damn, he is so cute and sexy." I say and perk my lips to the side.

"Did you get his number?" she asks with her hands on her hips.

"No, it's not like that," I say and take a swallow of my mellow-yellow drink.

"All right, somebody else is going to get that meat," Melody says as she stands beside her Mitsubishi Mirage stomping the dirt off her white, Air Force One tennis.

"I have to go now, football practice is almost over," I say trying to leave before Melody put something together that's not suppose to be.

"I'll call you later, so we can talk," Melody says as I drive off.

The little conversation with Melody has opened the door for more conversation. I tried to ease the question about Henry in a quick and slick manner, but Melody is on game when it comes to slick questions.

"Hey, baby. How was practice today?" I ask my son Flip as I meet him at the football gate behind the school.

Flip is a number one, football fan. He is twelve years old and has been on the starter line every since he was eight years old. I'm delighted to say that he gives it his best with making good grades in school and with his outstanding performance on the football field.

"Yes, ma'am, I had a good time at practice. I scored a touchdown," he says with excitement.

"That's wonderful," I say kissing him on his forehead. After spring practice is over, you'll be good and ready for the fall season. Here, put your helmet and shoes in the trunk. I have a bottle of water for you in the car," I say.

"I'm about to starve. Can we stop by Churches Chicken? I want me a three-piece combo," Flip says and take a drink of his water.

"I was going to go home and cook you your favorite meal. You know, fried chicken, white rice, scramble eggs, biscuits with grape jelly.

"Ma, I can't wait on that, I'm real hungry," he said.

"Fasten your seat belt, and drank all your water," I say and place my tray on the back seat of the car.

"Mamma, what you ate?" Flip asks.

"Oh, I ate hot wings and fries from the restaurant. It was good, but really hot."

We have to pass by Churches Chicken before we get home, so if that's what Flip wants to eat, then that's what he will eat. And it's a relief for me that I don't have to cook. I thought.

"How's your chicken?" I ask.

"Good ma," he says and drinks his Sprite.

"Don't forget to get your helmet and shoes out of the trunk," I say as I walk up the door steps.

I love everything about my brick home except my door steps. If I'm not careful, I'll fall and burst my ass. In the future my plans are to have them replace fuller and longer with sparkling rhinestones in a circler motion.

I open the door, and the first thing I hear is my phone ringing off the hook. I rushed and threw down my purse and keys to answer it.

"Hello," I answer.

"Girl, let me tell you what happen," Melody says.

If Melody says she is going to call, I better expect a phone call. It's a forty percent chance that what Melody has to talk about is good and beneficial, but it is also a sixty percent chance that it's just plan out negative. I should have checked the I.D. box before picking up the phone, because now just isn't a good time for me to talk.

"Girl, I have to call you back. I need to make sure I have everything out of the car," I say.

"I need to talk. It want take but a minute, I promise," she says.

"Ok, what's up?" I ask.

"I'm through this time. I'm so sick and tired of his ass. Every time his cell phone ring, he doesn't answer it when we are together. So when we got through fucking, he took a shower. While he was in the shower I checked his phone. The name I see in his phone leaving him a text message is Erica.

Hey, baby, I really enjoyed last night. The kids are fine this evening. I just want you to know that my pussy is all yours, and I need you tonight so we can do the remix. That's the message she left.

"After reading the message, I transformed into a raging beast. I walk my big ass in that bathroom. You talking about mad. I was mad. I slung that shower curtain open, and threw his little, naked, black ass up against the wall.

'Rodney! You still fucking yo kids mama!' I said holding him against the wall. I had a butcher knife at his neck with one hand, and the cell phone in my other hand showing him the text message.

'Nah, girl, what in the hell are you talking about?' his ass said, trembling like a mother fucker."

"Hold on, girl, wait a minute," I say stopping her.

My mind is not focus on Melody right at this moment, because Flip is too quiet. And when I can't hear or see him or know where he is at, I lose concentration immediately.

"Flip," I call.

"Huh," he answers tiredly.

As long as I heard his voice and he is ok, he could have yelled cock-a-dooly doo…it would have been fine with me.

"Did you get everything that needed to be out the car, out?" I ask.

"Yes, ma'am," he says walking into the living room and then crashing on the sofa.

"Ok. I'm back," I say to Melody.

'This text message is what the hell I'm talking about. You call her on this phone right now and tell her to stop calling you, and that you are just going to do for your kids and that's all, or get yo shit and leave.' I said holding the knife and phone all together. I eventually eased up and gave him the phone, so he could call.

'I need to dry off and put some clothes on first. We need

to talk about this in a more proper manner," he said.

"While he dried off, he talked about how much he loves me and that him and Erica relationship is strictly about their kids. 'I don't know why she is leaving messages on my phone. I want to be with you, why you don't believe me?' he said very coolly.

'Ok, you got your clothes on. I need you to prove to me that nothing is going on. Here is the phone, so call," I said as I passed him the phone.

'I'm not about to call that girl!' he screamed and was limping back and forth as he talk. 'I told you who I want,' he said putting his hands on my shoulders and trying to kiss me.

"Linda, I'm just not fallen for his lies anymore so I said, 'Get the hell out! You're lying! You weren't working late last night. You were with that bitch! Get out!' I scream and almost had an asthma attack. So I had to cool myself down and get me a glass of water.

'Ok. I'll leave; but remember when I'm gone, you want find no other man like me,' He said confidently.

"I threw him out with his clothes behind him," Melody says hysterically while breathing loud in the phone.

I held the phone in silence as I sit at my kitchen table. *This shit has been going on ever since I've known her and is getting worse,* I thought sadly.

"Damn, that's some thick shit. I'm glad I don't have that problem. I'm single and drama free. If you're with a man, and he causes you so much pain, it's time to do what's best for you. I'm waiting on God to send me the right man. Maybe you should do the same thing," I say.

"Every since you joined that Baptist Church you ain't been the same. What in the hell them folks done to you? You've change," Melody says hesitantly.

"To me, I'm still the same ordinary Linda, but, girl, for some strange reason I feel like it's a double person inside of me!"

It's time now for you to stop listening to her. Listen to her she's your friend, the voice begin to play over and over again in Linda ear.

"Ha…ha…ha, yo ass is really crazy. You need to get a SSI check, talking about you hear a double person," Melody laughs.

"Shit, I'm for real," I say shaking my head and staring at my decorative plates that sit in the center of my dining table. One person be saying, *What's up I'm Linda, but they call my Lee-Lee,* and be popping a piece of big, red, chewing gum. The other person says, *hello, my name is Linda Lax. It's a pleasure to meet you,* and continues to read a book. Girl, I can't explain it, but I do know trying to control the two ain't easy or fun. However, I have realized that there is a time and a place for everything," I explain.

"That's all I wanted to tell you," Melody says in lost of interest.

"What do you have plan for the rest of the evening?" I ask.

"I'm gonna pack my bags and go spend a few days with my brother Melvin in Birmingham, Alabama. Girl, he's a police officer now?" Melody says slightly laughing.

"Really, Melvin doesn't look as if he would want to be a police," I say in disbelief.

"Melvin came home early from work a year ago. He caught his baby mama in bed with a known drug dealer. The drug dealer whipped my brother ass. After that my brother began to hate anything and anybody who looks or act like a drug dealer. I believe that he thinks by being a police, he can punish somebody else for his pain from the ass whipping, and losing his baby mama to a drug dealer. He and I know that his ass is too scary to be a police, but he say he loves his job," Melody says.

"That's a serious job, and he needs to take it serious. His life can be on the line when trying to stop crime, especially if it's just for his own personal problem," I say seriously.

"He has been asking me to come and visit him every since he brought him a new house. Right now, I need a get-away," Melody says.

"Yeah you do," I say encouragingly.

"I'll holla later, girl," Melody says and hangs up.

CHAPTER 5

Wednesday Morning

Having my own shop is the best thing that could have happen to me. It keeps me occupied and focus. It's a challenge, but I love to challenge myself. Yes, I must say I feel like I have succeeded in my business and need to expand myself for my next challenge. Although, hair is my life, sometimes I get bored with the same thing every day. I find myself having to grow with my business in order to continue to be satisfied.

When I first started doing hair, I never imagine having my own shop, it just happened. Two ladies before me had a beauty salon. They later begin to hate one another. Courtney, who was the head owner in charge, hired me as a booth rental.

Swallowing the Lump

She constantly talked about Denise. Denise and Courtney were friends, which had led to them both opening the business together. Denise talked about Courtney all day when she wasn't working, and vice versa. I didn't know them like that, or wanted to hear the bull shit. I was just delighted to be working. Each time I had to hear and not hear, so I didn't know what to say, but, "Ah, oh, for real, well, it'll get better," I sometimes believe that that was too much to say. More often I just waved my head from side to side and thinking, *what have I gotten myself into?*

I was new in the business fresh out of beauty school and didn't have a clue to how things work. They weren't very good role models, and thank God, they didn't last three months after I started work. Denise left first and then Courtney. I begged for Courtney to stay, because with my booth rent and her booth rent we could pay the bills. Courtney just wanted out. As I pack my belongings to leave I thought sadly, *How could I be out of my first job.*

Strangely, a short, white man with curly hair walked into the building just when I was almost done packing. He asked who was I, and I told him Linda Lax. He introduced himself and told me that he was the owner of the building. He asked me if I would stay, and he would provide all the equipment for me to work, and all I had to do was pay him a weekly booth rent. That was the best offer I had every heard at the time. He was nice and quick to set the building up so that I wouldn't miss any time off work. I was working by myself with no drama, and business was off the chain. People were coming in from every angle there was. Then one day, the owner said, he wanted to rent another booth. I was like, ok, cool, but find somebody who wants to work. I was still fresh to the business, and all I was concern about was my clients and all the good money that I was making. Blossom got started, but there was a catch to the whole deal that slipped passed me like lighting that was never discussed. The shop license and my own beauty license were in my name. Therefore, I'm the manager, but the owner did the hiring and collected the booth rental fee. Nevertheless, I was just happy to work and didn't think about the future.

Blossom was good at the beginning until she got a bit too cocky. I couldn't tell her what to do, not even clean up her mess. I mean, I'm cool, but let's clean up behind ourselves, because either way it goes when inspection pops in, I'm the one who will get written up if things are not by the book. Blossom was very sassy, but not the real bitch sassy as me. Thank God, I learned to bite my tongue and control myself. My clients were important to me. I experienced by being professional, I could eat forever and keep clients coming.

The owner was never around, because he didn't live in the area. Things started to go downhill. I had pressure on me that I wasn't ready for and didn't know quite how to handle. Blossom knew that I wasn't her boss. She came in when she got ready, unfortunately, which was her money, you know, but when she came, she occupied company that wasn't getting their hair done. I mean—what the fuck, those are money chairs everybody knows that there are no unbeneficial loitering especially during business. I know she was just herself and that company is entertainment, but loiters ain't going to pay no bills. I mean you can learn a lot from other people, but you can also get cocky a little too fast. I was very attentive in beauty school. I learned by watching the owner, the instructor, the books, and the demonstrations. I had learned to be myself and a professional at work, and myself and myself at home. I wanted Blossom to be happy, comfortable and make money, so I continued to say nothing. As I was doing the silent phase, I was thinking a whole lot. I took what was going on and learned form it. I later stepped out on faith and got my own beauty salon. Now, I do things my way and my way.

"Hello, Linda Styling Salon. How may I help you?" I answer the shop phone.

At work clients come first. Focusing on and satisfying them is all about running a good business to me.

"Yes, my name is Jessie. You gave me a card at the restaurant. I would like to make an appointment for Friday," she says.

"How's Friday morning at eight?" I ask.

"That will be great," Jessie says and hangs up the phone.

"Excuse me, is the owner in?" two guys say after walking in the shop wearing purple, gold shirts with black jeans.

"Yes, she's over there on the phone," Co-Co says as she walks to empty her manicure bowl.

Co-Co is the nail tech. No other salon wants to hire Co-Co, because of her messy reputation. I told Co-Co, "Pay me on time, bring business to the shop, and leave anything beside business in the streets; and if there is a problem with us, I want you to bring it to me. If you can handle that, you got yourself a job."

A year and a half has passed since I first hired Co-Co and I must say she is a hard and dedicated worker.

"Can we hang a flyer in your window?" one of the guys asks.

"What type of flyer?" I ask as I held my hand out to read the flyer.

"It's about the College Greek Show we're having on Saturday night, and following the show is the after-party at Club Red on Marcuse Street," the short guy announces and scratches his corn rows.

"We have to go to the show!" Co-Co says and jumps up to read the paper.

"Sure, you can hang it up in the top window to your right," I say to the guys as I sit underneath the dryer to dry my roller set.

"Girl, this is the last show for the season until schools starts back in the fall. Come on, we can go together," Co-Co says.

Co-Co didn't know about my personal life and why going to the club isn't a quick jump-off for me anymore.

After I got my license to do hair, Melody and I went to Club 225 to celebrate. We clubbed every weekend with no problems until that particular night. Melody got into a fight with the security guard for trying to sneak a bottle of Seagram Gin in her bra.

"Girl, I don't like gin; it gets me drunk. I'm drinking vodka and pineapple juice at the bar," I said as I park the car behind the club.

"Look, I'm gonna sneak this gin in my bra, so I want have to buy nothing," Melody said and drank five swallows of the gin.

I shook my head and laughed.

"I'm just gonna pay my way in. Guys are always standing around the bar waiting to buy you a drink," I said, convincingly hoping that she will leave her gin in the car.

Melody and I walked to the door. The security guard was standing tall, bald-headed, and ready. I paid my ten dollars and got search, everything was fine. Melody walks in behind me and say, "I paid already."

I couldn't believe she had said that. I pinch my lips to the side hoping the lady would believe the lie.

"Ma'am, you didn't pay," the owner girl friend says as she holds her hand out of the payment window.

"Oh, yes, the hell I did pay!" Melody yelled.

"Ma'am you need to pay!" the security guard yelled.

He stops Melody by slightly grabbing her arm as she reaches to open the entrance door. Melody pushed the security guard shoulder and her gin fell to the floor.

"Oh, hell, nah!" Melody said as she looks down at her gin burst and spills all over the floor.

"Bang, a loud sound," she pushed the security to the wall.

The security guard rise up, and push Melody from the

front door to the side walk without any hesitation. I ran out to the side walk.

"Are you all right?" I asked trying to help her get up.

I was down with Melody but not down enough to fight a man, especially that security guard.

"Leave, before I call the police and don't bring y'all ass back here no more!" The owner rushed out the club and said without giving me my money back. I was too embarrassed and never went to Club 225 again.

"I haven't been out in two years," I say to Co-Co as I scooted emotionally in the drier chair.

"A little fun won't hurt," Co-Co says.

My curiosity is getting the best of me especially as Co-Co assures me that a little fun won't hurt.

"Well, I don't know about the Greek Show, but I'll meet you at Club Red for the after party, if Mama babysits for me," I say.

CHAPTER 6

I'm sitting at the bar, dinking on my second Bud Light, and enjoying the new single by Erykah Badu. Looking around I see that the crowd is more of the younger crew. I feel a little out of place, but seeing older guys I know makes me feel a little balanced. Watching Albert as he walks to the bar towards me makes me think of the reason why I didn't talk to him. Albert is biracial. His skin is a light, brownish red; and his hair is a sandy, medium texture. Albert offered to take me to dinner once, but as soon as he opens his mouth his breath smelt like a dumpster. The scent choked me, because it went down my throat. I tried to stand still and play the situation off, but I had to cough. I turned his offer down by lying that I had a man. He is fine and cute, but I love to kiss; and if I can't see myself kissing him, then it just can't be.

"Hello, Linda. How are you tonight?" Albert asks.

"I'm fine," I say wiggling my feet.

"What you doing out tonight all by your pretty little self?" he asks.

"I'm waiting on someone," I say and look at his wedding ring on his finger.

I turn my head to look for Co-Co, but she is nowhere in sight.

"You know, I really care about you and my offer still stand," he says and walks off.

Yeah, and your breath still stinks, I say to myself smiling while popping my gum and waving him a good-by.

"Hey, you finally made it," Co-Co says as she eased between two chairs and sit at the bar beside me.

"It's some nigga's in here tonight. No heifer in here should go home single tonight," she says popping her finger and her chewing gum.

"Ooooool," Co-Co moans. "I—I see who I'm looking for standing over there in that corner. Come, I want to introduce you," Co-Co says as she pulls her mini skirt up a little higher and arches her back before she began to walk.

"Wait, let me finish my beer," I say and turn the bottle up.

"Don't walk so fast. My pumps are too high, and I'ma trip and fall if I walk any faster," I say as I pull my jeans up to make sure my ass is sitting right.

"Jodie, this is Linda. Linda this is my friend Jodie," Co-Co introduces us.

"Hi, it's nice to meet you," Jodie speaks.

Jodie is the guy Co-Co talks about everyday nonstop.

"Hi, it's nice to meet you, too," I say.

"Co-Co, I'm going to the restroom," I say trying to get away from the both of them.

I can't believe that's the Jodie Co-Co has been talking about. His wife is my favorite, every week client. Shit, I don't want to know anything or hear his name at the shop again, I thought to myself.

"Hey, girl, I thought you had gotten lost in here," Co-Co says after walking into the restroom.

"No, but I'm glad you are in here. I didn't know that's the Jodie you've been talking about. He's married to Sidney, my client. Didn't you know that?" I ask.

"Yeah, but they are not together, that's what he told me," she says.

You silly rabbit, tricks are for kids, I thought to myself while staring at her. "Well, I don't know about all that. You need to keep his name out of the shop. Whatever you do in your personal life is cool, but remember, my clients are my money," I say.

"No one knows about us, but you," Co-Co assures.

"And now I'm telling you since I know, I don't want to know," I say.

Co-Co stands with her hands on her face and say, "I'm sorry, don't be mad at me."

"I'm not mad, but keep it between y'all," I say and give her a hug.

"I have church in the morning, I'm gonna leave," I say as

Swallowing the Lump

I look in the mirror glossing up my lips.

"You need me to walk outside with you?" she asks.

"No girl, I'm not scared," I say as we leave the restroom.

I don't give a damn who man Co-Co fuck, but that's too close to my pocket. And I need every penny I make and then some. I can't let her jeopardize me. Now, I got to feel guilty every time I do Sidney hair, because I know Co-Co is fucking her husband. When the shit boils down, I ain't got a damn thing to do with it.

I'm standing at the front door to exit the club, but more of the Greek Show crowd is coming in. The exit entrance is closed and now I have to wait to get out through the main entrance. I tip-toe momentarily to see how long the crowd stand, and it's a medium wait.

Oh shit, that looks like Henry walking in, I smile thinking to myself.

I don't know if Henry remembers me from the restaurant or not, so I stood still behind a high table to see if he's alone. Two more guys walk through the door behind him. I see Henry staring my way. I'm getting butterflies in my stomach. I turn my face, so that he couldn't get a good look, and I walk out the door.

Seeing Henry for the second time made chills run all the way through my body. Unlocking my car door, I contemplate about going back inside to sit at the bar. *Perhaps we can have a nice little conversation,* I thought charmingly.

Unfortunately, I'm home lying in bed forcing myself to sleep. I'm so forced. I'm tossing from side to side and kicking my feet. I just can't take it anymore. I get up and search through my C.D. stand. I see my R. Kelly C.D., *Chocolate Factory.* Placing it into the stereo I skip through and press play on his song, "Imagine That." I turn the radio on low, hoping it'll relax me. I lay down, but listening to the music made me think about Henry. I'm really, really forced and can't sleep at all. I need to get this pressure off of me, or I'm gonna go nuts.

I reach into my bottom dresser drawer and grab one of my sex toys. My butterfly always comes in handy. I strap, the back straps around my back. I pull the right strap up my right leg to my inner thigh, and the left strap up my left leg to my inner thigh. I take off my peach slip and drop it to the floor. I gently lie on my back. I spread my legs wide with the butterfly centered in the middle on my clitoris. I'm relaxed and visualizing myself on top of Henry with my knees on the bed and my legs folded between his thighs. My breast is resting against his chest with my hands pressing off the head board. I'm riding him, slithering like a loose lizard until his veins pops out the temple of his forehead. "Sssss…" I say as I speed the butterfly a little faster.

"Oh shit! Henry. Henry. Henry oh shit!" I scream.

Damn that was good, I say to myself and unbutton my butterfly scraps to wash my hands, clean myself, and my toy.

I jump back in bed to cuddle in my sheets, but damn, a wet spot. I'm not getting back up, so I toss the bottom sheet on the floor, and wrap myself into my top sheet and fluffy, king-size comforter.

I set my alarm clock for 8:00 a.m. and crash instantly.

Swallowing the Lump

★★★★★★

Early the next morning my alarm clock goes off as usual. I stretch and take a shower.

Where is my slip? I know I laid it somewhere last night, I wonder.

I crawl on my knees butt naked on the floor around my bed until I found my slip. I put my slip on and began down the hall to the kitchen, and my phone ring.

"Hello," I answer.

"Good morning, are you up?" Mama asks.

"Yes, Mama, I'm up. How are you this morning?" I ask.

"I'm good," Mama says.

"Is Flip ready?" I ask.

"Yes baby, we've been up since 7:00," she says.

"I'll be over in a little bit, after I finish cooking me some breakfast," I say.

Mama always calls me the next morning when she knows I've been to the club. She's very concern. If she wasn't asleep when the club closes, I think she would call me after I get home from the club.

I remember one night, late after the club I was kinda wooly, and went to the Travel and Dine restaurant for a bite to eat. Soon as I arrive at the restaurant, the park-in-lot was extremely crowded. I got excited, and wanted to see what was going on. I anxiously found a park, and jump out of the car. I eagerly locked my keys inside the car. I knew that my hands were too empty, but it was too late, my keys were on the seat.

I panic when I saw the police arriving to clear the park-in-lot. I considered myself as being too wooly, and might go to jail if I had asked the police for help. Nonetheless, I went inside the restaurant, and call Mama for the extra set of car keys. Without a doubt and considering that it was 3:00 in the morning, Mama came to my rescue. I felt irresponsible and dense headed after calling Mama that time of the morning. Unpredicted, Mama followed me all the way home. However, I thought Mama was going to lead the way, and let met follow her, but she told me to get in front. That was the most I ever concentrated while driving. I was using signal lights on ever turn even if it was just a curve turn. I watched both lines on the road, the white line and the yellow line making sure that I stayed in between both. Concentrating nervously at the stop sign I made sure that I came to a complete stop. I looked right for a couple of seconds, and then I looked left for a couple of seconds. Standing at the door fumbling with my keys to get inside, Mama just sat in her car with her lights shining on me. She blew her horn and left as I walked in.

"Heeeeeey, I bought some bacon and egg biscuits for everyone," I say and take the biscuits to the kitchen.

"Mama, it's really hot in here," I say wiping my forehead.

"I cook my cornbread on top of the heater this morning," Mama says.

This morning, I just can't sit still and talk to Mama. I want to, but my exhaustion from the club, alcohol, and my self-masturbation is all teaming together with this heat having my head beginning to spin in circles.

Swallowing the Lump

"Mama, we have to go. I'm on program at church today. We'll be back after church for some dinner," I say.

"What you rushing for gal? You have plenty of time before church starts," Mama says walking Flip and me to the door.

"We have to get dress. We'll be back," I say rushing out the door.

★★★★★★

I made it to church early enough to read over the program and to unwind. Thinking and contemplating is making me nervous. I go to the ladies' room and tell myself to calm down and stop thinking negative. I hurriedly arrive back to my seat, and read the program studiedly.

Worship & Invocation: #123 Pastor Calmly

Devotion: Choir Members & Deacons

Selection: # 124 Choir & Congregation

Responsive Reading: #595 led by Sis. Linda Lax

I did just fine. I just took a deep breath with determination. I began to reading like I read and got out of my Blue Tail Horse Book in third grade.

"Hello Ms. Smith, good to see you back and doing well," I say and give her a hug after shaking Pastor Calmly hand at the end of service. Ms. Smith is the Director of the Usher Board. She's been on bed rest due to her severe arthritis.

"Baby, you look good. I want you and that boy of yours to stay in church now, you hear," Ms. Smith says.

"Yes, ma'am, we will," I say leaving with a smile on my face.

Preparing myself for the program not only made me nervous, but also worked up a huge appetite. It seems as if can smell Mama cooking a mile away.

"The food was delicious Mama," I say and kiss her on her lip.

"Sorry we can't stay a little longer," I say to Mama after spending two hours sitting and talking with her. "I promise Mrs. Selma, I will come over her house to trim her split ends," I say.

Mrs. Selma is my next door neighbor. Every time she bakes a pound cake, she sends me a slice. Mrs. Selma use to own her own bakery until she got up in age and couldn't stand, because her knees bother her so bad. She still bakes for a few people in town for extra money. Since we don't have a lot of restaurants here in Yazell, everybody cooks or knows someone who can cook. If you're not careful you'll be overweight from all of the soul food.

It's a relief to get home and pull off these heels and stocking. My baby toe was hurting from the heels last night, but now it's throbbing. When I'm not careful, I always bump my baby toe at the edge of my coffee table or at the corner of my sofa. My toe takes forever to heal.

"Ma, we're out of Kool-Aid," Flip says while standing in the refrigerator holding the pitcher.

"Ok, baby," I say as I put my white clothes in the washing machine.

Swallowing the Lump

"Come on, we're going to The Something Valuable Grocery Store. We need some grocery," I say after I finish putting the clothes in the laundry. I grab my purse and keys and we head out the door.

"Grandma was on the phone with Mrs. Mayo and said, "Something Valuable have a good sale on grocery this week," Flip says.

Mrs. Mayo and Mama are best friends. She and Mama use to hang at the pool hall together. They talk on the phone occasionally than they see each other in person.

"Are you listening to Mama's phone conversations?" I ask opening the car door.

"No, Ma, we were all in the living room watching Walker Texas Ranger, and Mrs. Mayo call Grandma, and I heard her talking," Flip explains.

"Hand me a sale paper off the buggy, and let me see what's on sale," I say. "Oh, this is dollar week. Pass me a bottle of Hunts Ketchup and a jar of Miracle Whip," I say.

"Hello their, how are you and your fine, young man doing today?" Mr. Macon asks.

"Whenever I see you, you look more and more like your grandmother. I saw y'all at service today, but y'all left before I could get over to you," he said.

"We are doing good, Mr. Macon. How have you been?" I ask.

"We'll, sugar, I want complain. I'm gonna say to you just like I say to everybody else. Love God, love yourself, be yourself; because no body is perfect. Remember that and you'll be all right," he says with one hand resting on my shoulders and the other hand in his pocket.

"I hope you and the rest of the children at church have fun on the trip to Disney World," he says looking at Flip as he stumbles and walks away.

Mr. Macon is the senior Deacon on the Deacon Board. He retired after teaching the school choir for thirty-six years. Even though he drinks his alcohol, Mr. Macon is a good man. He always parks at the Quick Service Gas Station in front of the Package Store, and wait for Big Man Tom to bring him a paint of Crown Royal. Mr. Macon wife belongs to another church across town. Mr. and Mrs. Macon are never seen together no more than if you pass by their house and see them on their front porch rocking in their rocking chairs.

"Baby put your seat belt on," I say to Flip.

Sitting at the traffic light waiting on the light to change, it looks as if I see Henry waiting at the light horizontally from me.

"Oh, my God, it is Henry," I start mumbling.

The traffic light turns green. Henry sees me, and he waves with a smile. I smile and start waving my hand out the window. *Every time I see Henry we are not able to talk. I want to talk or say something,* I thought.

"Who's that mama waving?" Flip asks and look back to see.

"Someone I went to high school with," I say and smile.

CHAPTER 7

July 2006

It's the 4th of July and business is going full speed. Thank God for the trip to Disney World. I needed that break. I'm more revived and energetic. I think I enjoyed myself more than the kids, because I rode all the rides and did everything pertaining to the trip. Some of the kids didn't want to ride or participate in activities; they just walk and looked. But not me, I enjoyed every minute of the trip.

"Hello, Jessie. How are you doing this morning?" I ask.

"I'm fine. I loved my hair, and it held up the entire two weeks. I was wondering if you could take me as a walk-in this morning. I have to be at work by two o'clock," Jessie says while rubbing her fingers through her hair.

"Sure, I can do your hair. I was waiting on a client, but

she called and said, she'll be a little late."

"Linda, how long have you been doing hair?" Jessie asks while I'm shampoo her hair.

"I've been doing hair for eight years," I say.

"Do you like it?" she asks.

"I love it, I'm my own boss," I say.

"Did you go to Beauty School, as soon as you finished high school?" she asks.

"No. When I finished school, I worked at several jobs before I decided to go to Beauty School. I worked at a hat factory, fish plant, and I waitress and cooked at the Travel and Dine restaurant where you work. I was gliding myself from job to job. If the Supervisor made me mad, I quit. If a holiday was coming up and I was on schedule to work when I requested to be off, I quit. Until my mother said to me, 'Every time you get a job and somebody makes you mad, you quit. You have a child, and you can't provide for him or yourself by quitting all these jobs. You're always in the mirror combing your hair, you comb my hair and my sister Claret hair when she's home from Georgia. Go to Hair School!'

Claret lived with us for a while when she was a teenager. I remember getting Claret in trouble once, and she didn't fool with me too much after then. Mama had gone to town and Claret was watching us. She was cleaning the house and I was bored. I wanted the broom she had so I could clean, too. Mama never let me clean up, because I didn't take my time to clean right. I didn't like to clean, but when Claret cleaned up it looked good and easy. We were on the porch and I wanted the broom, so I took it from her and Claret snatched it back. I was standing at the edge of the porch, and we were pulling the broom back and forth. Claret let go, and I fell off the six-foot porch onto a long, rusty nail. The nail went through the bottom of my foot and stuck out through the side of my foot. Claret helped me up off the ground. She helped me inside the house and made me a pallet on the floor. My foot was swelling and bleeding seriously, and every time I looked at my foot I cried louder. Dreadfully, I kinda knew that it was my fault what had happen to me. However, Claret was scared, because when Mama gave a whipping she gave a whipping. Mama came home and as soon as Kendrick said, "There go Mama," I burst out to crying even more. Mama came in the house and saw me lying on the floor with my foot on a bloody towel and pillow. I told Mama Claret push me off the porch, and I burst out to crying. Mama punished Claret good. She wasn't able to anywhere for a whole month. Mama doctored on me herself, and my foot healed up in weeks. I was kinda sorry for what I did, but all Claret had to do was give me the broom.

Claret didn't fool with or say a word to me much, especially when I wanted my way. She'll just say, I'm gonna tell on you, or you go back home and don't follow me. I didn't have any friends, and Claret didn't let me go nowhere she went. Each time she went around the corner to her friend house, I still followed her. I'll stop and sit at the edge of the road where she could see me and wait for them to have a boy come over. Although they were just ordinary neighborhood boys that would stop by I was mad and still made a big issue out of it.

Swallowing the Lump

Sometimes a boy or two would come and sit on the porch with them, and sometimes they didn't; but when they made fun of me and laugh because I couldn't sit on the porch, I'll run home and tell my Mama over and over again that Claret is being fast. Sometimes, I lied just so she could come home.

"Tell Claret I said come here," Mama said.

I was so happy to hear Mama say those words. I'll run around the corner full speed and stop at the stop sign and scream, "My Mama said come home," Claret was mad and walked ahead of me with her arms folded up. I walked behind her with a smile on my face. Claret eventually moved back to Georgia and got married. She and I now sit back and laugh at the way I use to be.

"I'm going to babysit Flip so you can go to beauty school," My Mama fussed. Mama was telling me the truth. So when Mama said, "I'm going to babysit," I knew I had better take that to an advantage, because Mama punished me good after I had Flip. All my freedom was taken away.

"Wherever I went, Flip had to go," I say to Jessie.

"The reason, I ask, I've been out of high school two years. I moved here from Jacksonville, Florida with my dad after him and my mom got a divorce. I didn't like my dad girlfriend, nor do I like my mom boyfriend, so I'm living on my own. My plan is to work and not go to college, but I'm not making enough money, I can barely pay my apartment rent," Jessie says sitting in my stylist chair as I roller set her hair.

"If I was you, I would go to school and get some type of trade. Whether it's for a year or two years, it's will be something that will help you get on your feet. It's a bus that comes about five miles from here to the Smith and Eddies' Flower Shop. It gives anyone who goes or wants to go to, The Fast Start Community College, a ride to and from school for just two dollars a day. The College is forty-five minutes from here, and it also offers financial aid. And I know that your job will work around your schedule. Try it, you'll like it," I assures and put her underneath the dryer.

The shop phone rings while I'm putting Jessie underneath the dryer.

"Hello, Linda Styling Salon," I answer.

"May I speak to Linda?" a lady says.

"This is she," I say.

"What's up chick, this is Amy. I called you last week to pay you back the money I owe you, but I didn't get an answer. You can come by this evening and get your money, I have it," Amy informs.

"Ok, that's cool I'll be over," I say.

"Oh, I almost forgot, will you bring me a case of Bush Beer by the house? I'll pay you for everything when you get here," she says.

Amy and I use to work at the hat factory together. Every since she fell at work and fractured her lower spine, she's being drawing her disability. She borrows a few dollars from me every now and then. She always pay me back a month later, but this particular time it's been four months. Hell, I forgot she even owe me.

The last time I was over Amy house, we had a good time

drinking beer and smoking weed reminiscing about the old days.

"Girl—" Cough…she chokes. "I use to fuck the school bus driver," Amy said and laughs.

"No shit. You're lying," I said laughing nonstop.

"The other kids were mad because he always let me off in front of my door instead of the bus stop," she said taking another pull.

"Damn you were a hot mama," I said slowing down the laughter. "Guess what? The police caught Patrick and me on top of his daddy car hood at the creek having sex. We were butt naked," I said laughing and holding my hands between my legs to keep from pissing on myself.

"When did this happen?" she asked breathlessly.

"Patrick and I went to the prom together. After the prom I had twenty minutes left before I had to be at home, so we went and parked at the creek," I said.

"What did the police do?" she asked laughing.

"He shined his flash light and told us to leave, or he was going to take us to the police station and call our parents," I said looking serious and cracking a smile at the same time.

Amy was on her knees killing herself laughing.

"Y'all didn't see or hear the police car," she catches her breath and asked.

"Hell, nah. We were on top of the hood, and the trunk was facing the dirt road. I wasn't thinking about a car or nobody else, I was just getting it on. I believe that's the night I got pregnant with Flip," I said.

Amy and I had a good time that night smoking weed and reminiscing about our life funniest and embarrassing moments. Unexpectedly, it was the next time that I went over to her house. Amy announced that she had some different weed. She said that the pain in her lower spine makes it hard for her to sleep at night and she needed something with a little more fire. Sometime, I think Amy is going to smoke her brain away, because I was straight and didn't need anything different.

"Different weed, what you mean different weed," I asked.

"It's some fire ass weed. I got it from Lil Sneak," she said while rolling the blunt.

"You know the only way I'm going to smoke, is if the weed came from old man Winston," I said sitting on the couch watching her temptingly as she rolls the blunt.

Winston is fifty-six years old. He always talks about how he's from the old school and how they use to party and dance all night. I liked that Winston was laid back and older, because his weed suited me just fine.

"Winston weed don't do nothing for me no more. The word is, Lil Sneak, weed is the shit. I had some earlier. It's the truth! You can handle it, trust me I know," she said convincingly.

Cough. Cough. She choked and passed the blunt to me.

Cough…Cough…Cough…Cough. I choked and passed her the blunt back quickly.

She took two pulls and passed the blunt back. The blunt was getting passed back and forth quicker than we ever passed.

"It's some good shit, isn't it?" she asked.

Swallowing the Lump

I took another pull and said, "This shit is strong. I'm done. I'm going home. I need to clean up."

The fifteen minute drive was the longest drive I had ever taken, where's to any other day it takes me five minutes. I'm so high, I can't think straight. My skin on my arms is beginning to tingle as I drive. I never felt like this before. I'm walking from one end of the house to another. I'm seeing ghost and hearing strange sounds. "My God, I'm so high. God, I have smoke this weed, I know you know, please help me get over this," I prayed.

I'm going crazy! I need to call my mama and tell her, "I got high over to Amy house, and I need her to take me to the E.R! Mama may panic or whatever, but I need her help. I don't know what to do. I think I need a shot!" I got a cold towel and washed my face four times. I hear something ringing constantly. I thought it was my brain—until I look at my house phone and saw the light flashing. I calm myself down to answer.

"Hello," I answer slowly.

"Hey, baby, I cook some chicken soup. Flip has already eaten. I cooked enough for you, too," Mama said.

Damn, I'm glad to hear her voice. I took a deep breath. I didn't tell Mama what was going on, but I kept her on the phone talking as long as I could to bring my high down.

"Ok, Ma, I'll be on over," I said and hung up the phone.

The high was wearing down. I opened a box of Nutty Buddies and ate one. I didn't know what kind of weed that was, but I almost went crazy. I took a cool shower and began to feel like myself again.

"Here's your money and keep the change," Amy says while wiping the top of her beer. "I got some good. You want to smoke?" she offers.

"No, girl, the last time I had a very bad experience. It's just not for me," I say.

Amy coughs and sat back in her chair laughing.

"Everybody have a bad experience. You should've stayed longer and let your high came down," she says and sips her beer.

"I don't know, but that shit almost fucked me up. I don't want shit, from nobody, who has little in the front of their name, or no one who even looks little. I'm serious, you better be careful with who you deal with!" I say.

CHAPTER 8

It doesn't seem like the holiday to me. Generally, I would be at the mall getting my nails done and buying me an outfit for tonight to hit the club later. Flip is with his dad and family for the weekend. They went to Georgia for their family reunion. All I plan to do is lie around the house and sleep. That is until my phone rings.

"Hello," I answer.

"Get up! Get up! Get yo ass up, or I'm coming to get you up! This damn club is off the chain. I have never seen Club Red this pack!" Melody screams.

"Are you for real?" I ask and stand to my feet.

"Hell, yeah, the whole town plus out of town visitors are in this club, except you," she says.

Melody knows how to hype me up even when I'm not

in the mood. I wasn't really sleepy and all I needed was that wake-up call.

"I'll be there in forty-five minutes," I say rushing to the shower.

Getting ready for the club doesn't take me a long time. I have all my club clothes on one side of the closet, and my everyday clothes on the other side with my church clothes in the middle. That keeps me well organized for any event.

My old dark denim Jeans that fits perfectly, and black halter top with silver rhinestones across my breast go together flawlessly; not to mention, my silver, Nine West, open-toes heels so the French tip on my toes can show, is my outfit for tonight. I'll spray a little Burberry around my wrists and neck, and I'm good to go.

"About time, you made it," Melody says.

"I've been here for ten minutes. I was in the rest room glossing my lips," I say posing by the bar. "You are right, Club Red is pack. I had to park across the train tracks at the old Relax and Stay Motel," I say excitedly.

"I just got off the dance floor doing the Bunny Hop," Melody says.

"I saw you as I walked past the dance floor," I say.

"Damn, that was a long song and dance," Melody says as she fans with a napkin.

"Did you come out by yourself?" I ask as we gets comfortable sitting at the bar.

"No, girl, I forgot to tell you, Rodney and I work things out, and we're planning to get married and have us a family," she says smiling.

"Is Erica out the picture?" I ask.

"Yes. The bitch skip town and went to Mamie, Florida. She got engaged to a man she met on the internet," Melody says looking relieve.

Melody and Rodney damn near ran Erica insane. A week ago Melody saw Erica at the service station, and pulled over to ask her why she is texting her man. Erica slapped Melody, and burst her bottom lip. They both were wrapped into one another like the snakes that were wrapped in the pit on the Anaconda movie. Neither of them was able to be pulled apart until the owner of the store threw cold water on them. Erica jump in her car, and speeded off. Melody jumped in her ride, and chased her. Melody drove close to Erica, and damn near ran her off the road. Melody threw a half full drink can at Erica car as she rode closely beside her, and cracked her window. It was that very moment while Erica drove frantically for her life and her kids' life as they slept unconsciously in their car seat to realize that Melody was crazy. The fighting, the lies and the back and forth shit Rodney was doing had literally cause Erica her job, and almost her life. It was too much for her to handle. Erica knew that she had to leave Yazell before Melody takes her, and her kids' life. She internet shopped and found her a man, rented a u-haul, and boned out.

"I'm so happy for you!" I say and stand up to give her a hug.

"Look," she says.

"Look where?" I ask.

109

"Over by the pool tables, Rodney is watching me, we're in love," she says.

We look his direction and wave cheerfully. I never imagine being comfortable out with Melody again at the club, because of what had happen at Club 225. I'm relaxed, and Melody has a smile on her face from ear to ear. We even got on the dance floor and dance to R. Kelly song, "Step In The Name Of Love."

"You remember the guy you say is so cute and sexy?" Melody asks screaming over the music.

"What!" I scream.

"The guy you say is cute and sexy," she scoots closer and screams.

"Yes. Henry," I say and look in her face.

"Don't turn around yet, but he's walking straight over here," she says cutting her eyes to one side.

I almost froze up, so I start talking to Melody as if we are in a deep conversation, distracting myself from being nervous in case he stops.

"Hello, ladies. How are y'all doing?" Henry speaks and gives us a hug.

"What's up?" Melody speaks.

"Hey," I speak with a slight smile.

"Can I buy you lovely ladies something to drink?" he asks generously.

"I'm straight," Melody says.

'What about you, Ms. Lady," he asks.

"A frozen strawberry daiquiri would be fine," I say in-

110

nocently.

"Henry has come a long way compared to years ago. He is sexy and cute. If you let him get away this time, you are most definitely going to miss out," Melody says looking me face to face with frowns in her forehead.

"I told you once before that I'm not in a hurry for a relationship. I'm waiting on God to send me someone," I say firmly and cross my leg.

"How or when are you going to know who God send you, if you don't date someone?" Melody asks.

"You know, Melody, I really believe in that equal shit. I know, we all need someone who knows and love God. Everybody says with a good and stable job, decent credit, and who carry themselves respectfully and etc. Those are things that I know for certain and hear, but I know myself and it's a feeling that you suppose to have the very moment you meet that person.

"You may try to hide and ignore the feeling. You might even go and choose who you want, and be in an incapable relationship with. Which we all know that someone is going to get burden down, after putting in their all, and not being fully satisfied whether it's mentally or physically. You know, just the shit that makes you say, 'What in the hell have I got myself into,' I mean, it's an indescribable feeling. For instance, good girl who don't have any street sense meet bad boy with street sense. They fall head in love, but in the core of their relationship things get unbalance. My point is, you can teach, pat, and build someone up to be the person for you; but when they learn, I mean really learn, things starts to ponder your third eye. You see a person that you never seen before come out of a cage. It's like they have taken your strength plus the strength they already had and becomes to powerful for you."

"What do you do, whip them and say, "Go back to your cage?" I ask hypothetically.

Melody looks at me as if I have taken her too far into another world.

"Now, what if bad boy change to good man. He was allowed to run wild repeatedly, but he manages to swing himself through the jungle by using his third eye and the limbs from the trees so he wouldn't fall into a trap. On the other hand, you're on foot running curiously wild, but is guided with your third eye to keep you from falling into a trap. Suddenly within a pause, the two meet. They are quickly connected happily together, and they skip down dream land to share their story," I pause and gaze.

"Hello, earth to Linda, earth to Linda. Come back to America. We live in America, remember," Melody says.

"Shit, I know where we live," I say as I lean my elbow on the bar.

"You know you really need to think deep, because I really believe in that shit," I say bumping against Melody with my elbow.

"I want someone I can feel safe with no matter what. Someone I can trust. Even though little lies are easy to tell, but some innocent lies I think are needed. For instinct, if my husband comes downstairs into my office and I'm working on my computer, I'm over-focus trying to get my project completed, and he asks, 'Honey, you like my new suit I have on? I saw it in Mr. Boss, and I had to buy it today," I don't like the color of the suite on him, but I take a good look at the suit and say with a smile, 'Yes, honey, it is beautiful and looks amazing on you," I may be wrong for lying, but one morning I may asks, 'Baby, do my breath stink?' My breath may smell like onions, but he say, "Baby, what you talking about, your breath don't stink at all. Do you think I will let you breathe in my face every night and morning if you had bad breath?" he would say.

"You feel me?" I ask looking at Melody and pause.

Melody looks confusingly at me and rolls her eyes.

"I want someone who is not to fast for me and not to slow. Someone who has my back and I have his, no matter what; you know like a balance me out thing. Someone who can look at me and say, 'I know what you are thinking,' or Something ain't right about you today, and the same with me about him.' I believe in that kinda shit. It's gotta be true, because every time I do it my way, I'm not happy," I say. "Sound crazy?" I ask.

"Yo ass dreams too much. Don't know fairy tales come true anymore," Melody says shaking her head from side to side.

"Ok, you'll see one day," I assure.

"Trust me; before I met Rodney, I've dated plenty of men. Having me a young tender piece of meat that I can tame my way is what make things that much easier. Now this day

113

and time you have to get in where you fit in, or be left out," she says and rolls her eyes.

"See, you like that dominate and miserable shit that has the tendency to backfire. I like my dream, and it's just something about that bad boy turns good shit I like. You don't dream?" I ask.

"Hell no, dreams don't come true," she says.

"If you believe in them, they will," I say.

I've been single for a couple of years. But, Melody didn't know how much I wanted Henry and dream of him every night for the past months. This isn't my decision, and controlling myself right now is hard, especially when I have someone in my corner telling me her opinion.

"I've been eager to see you again. I was wondering if I can get your number and call you sometime," Henry says as he gives me my daiquiri.

I sip my daiquiri on that thought, and before I can say a mumbling word Melody is giving me a pen and a napkin.

"Here, you can write on this," she says smiling.

Looking at Melody with a sneaky, I'm-going-to-cut-your-throat look, I immediately write my numbers on the napkin and hand it to Henry.

"What's the best time to call?" Henry asks.

"Anytime is fine," I say looking him into his eyes.

"Drinks are on me, so you lovely ladies enjoy yourselves and have a wonderful night," he says and walks to the pool table.

My imagination is getting the best of me as Henry walks

away. I should have passed the phone call up, but it's a force on the inside of me that is beating the shit out of me, and screaming Henry. I just know that when I get my hands on him, it's going to be O.V.

"Hey! Wake up. Yo ass will drift off in a heartbeat. See that wasn't so bad," Melody says bumping me with her elbow.

"No it wasn't, but I'm sticking to my word," I say sticking a piece of big red chewing gum in my mouth.

"What's up Linda?" Rodney speaks and leans on the back of Melody chair as if his limp has gotten the best of him.

"Hey," I speak back.

"You ready?" he asks Melody.

"Girl I'll holler later," Melody says smiling and walks off.

I'm happy that Melody is happy. It feels good to know that what she has been through in her life, she's now finally happy. I pray for good results between her and Rodney, but from this day forward she's on her own. I need to get on with what's ahead for my life. Following Melody, I feel as if I put myself on hold. Now I'm lost, but the strangest thing, I feel like 60 pounds has been lifted off of me.

CHAPTER 9

Melody said something that stayed on my mind from the moment I left the club, and even as I fix me a turkey sandwich, and sit down on my sofa. It's been two years since I've given anyone a chance, and maybe I do dream too much. My dream world allows me to block out reality and visualize existence. I sometimes feel behind, because I'm now only fulfilled with watching *Fred Sanford & Son and I Love Lucy.* For the simple fact is that my interest in watching up-to date movies and T.V. shows got lost years down the road somewhere. Thinking back, I remember just where I left off. It was the Fresh Prince of Bel-Air. Will Smith character is very hilarious to me, I was eager to watch the show, but since his transition, and my pastime, I lost the years in between to watch movies that he's apart of. I use to think as a fan that you like a person because of the character that they play, and that's the person whom they are. I remember the first time when the movie, I Robot was coming to theaters soon and starting, Will Smith, I was like, what, and who in the hell is a, I Robot. I don't know him. That's not the person who plays on The Fresh Prince of Bel-Air, or is the Artist who sings "Summer, Summer, Summer Time." So, now as I sit and think I must be behind and if I don't fast forward and get into Robots, Mars, Jupiter, and gold, Space Ships, I'm really going to be left out. However, until you understand transition, and growth, you may at a point to become less interested in the people who have. Soon, I'm going to purchases I Robot, and all of his movies, so that I can catch back up, and enjoy all the new characters that he now and has played over the years.

Continuing to eat my turkey sandwich it's beginning to taste sour as I sit and remember my last two relationships. Anthony was a guy I started dating after Patrick and I broke up. I met Anthony at the Public Library here in Yazell, Alabama. He was on the investment and financial aisle. Anthony was a short, brown-skinned man who always dressed professionally. He taught me a lot about investing and finances, but besides the teaching something just wasn't clicking for us. He worked out of town and came home two weeks out of the month and most holidays. Now, the working out of town I can understand. Jobs are to a minimum here in Yazell. The thing that bothered me the most when I called him, he never answers, unless I called him at work. I knew if I called his job, he had to answer. We dated for eight months until my mind began to wonder.

"I've been calling you all week. You haven't checked your phone," I said being as calm as I could be.

"Oh, baby, my cell phone doesn't pick up when I'm in a bad location. Is everything all right?" he explained and then asked.

"Sure everything is cool," I said slowly nodding my head up and down.

"I thought you were coming home for Thanksgiving, and since it is the Monday after Thanksgiving, I wouldn't have heard from you unless I called. What's up, Anthony? I'm getting a funny vibe," I said.

"Baby, nothing is up, I've just been working hard, and that's all. Baby, I'll be home soon after I finish this job. I'll be home for a whooooooole month to give you some of this good loving. I promise; Okay." he said pathetically.

I held the phone quietly.

"Okay. Sweetie, I can't heaaaaaaar you" he said softly dragging his voice.

"Okay," I said with frowns, thinking of how his bumping and moaning of loving makes me sick to my stomach.

"I love you. I'll call, when I get off," he said making three kissing sounds in the phone.

Anthony didn't call for three days. I sat on my sofa and began to wonder, what was really going on. I only had his cell phone number and his work number. I was curious to know whether or not he had a home phone, so I called Information to see.

"What city, and state please?" Information asked.

"Dallas, Texas," Information said.

"What listing?" Information asked.

"Anthony Moonlight," I said.

"I have a Melissa and Anthony Moonlight. Hold for the number," Information said.

I listen for the number and called the number as soon as I hung up with Information.

"Hello. You have reached the Moonlight family, we're not home. Please leave a message, and we'll call you back as soon as possible," the answering machine said.

Now, at that particular moment, I was mad as hell. I wanted to call and tell his wife everything. I wanted to curse him out and call him everything, except a child of God. I had to do some serious thinking.

I'm only going to make myself look, sound, and feel bad if I call his home.

I began to fault myself just as much as I faulted him, because I didn't give myself a chance to get to know him before thinking I was in a relationship. I needed to think things thoroughly out my way, without saying another word to Anthony. Anthony called me persistently and I didn't answer.

A month had passed, and without expectation, in the dark, cold, misty air, Anthony was outside my house knocking at my door. I ran to the back end of my house and called the police.

"There is a man outside my door harassing me! Please

hurry! I need help, hurry!" I screamed through the phone in a whispering voice.

I hung the phone up and let Anthony see me peep out of the curtains as if I was coming to answer the door. The police arrived in no time.

"Help me! I'm afraid of him. He's being beating on my door all night," I open the door and lied to the police crying.

Anthony had just left the bar and had him one to many drinks that night. The police gave him an alcohol test. It proved that his alcohol level was three times over the limit. The police arrested him for public intoxication, disorderly conduct and harassment. Boy did I sleep good that night!

★★★★★★

My natural instincts guided me to satisfying myself sexually, so sex wasn't my main concern. I began to meditate a lot to myself wanting to know what I'm looking for in a man besides his rhythm. Patrick and I dated during and after high school; when I think about us, we didn't know anything about a relationship. We were just exploring. Over the years, I am proud to say I can finally speak to Patrick and be in the same presence with him for our son sake. I consider myself being a good and respectful mom. I am hard working and all of the above, but when it comes to men I always pick who I want instead of waiting on God.

It all takes me back when Mama said to me, "I wasn't ready for a relationship especially moving in with a man, but I did it my way anyhow. I got my own apartment when I was 20. To me, I was grown and had a son, so I was ready to play mommy and daddy. It was certain things we couldn't do in mama house especially sitting on the sofa with a guy as if I'm on a date.

Mama didn't allow boys over to her house. Everyday I went to school and talk about my make-believe boyfriend and his grandma. He lived out of town in New York City. His grandma lived in my neighborhood, and he came to visit her every summer. I always talked about how I cook, and comb the make-believe grandma hair, and that she'll let me drive her car anywhere I wanted to go. The story was so easy for me to tell, because all I did every morning when I got on the school bus was think about what I was going to say next about my make-believe boyfriend. Through elementary and middle school we didn't have a lot for entertainment. No cable television or a phone. However, once a week our class went to the library to check out a book of your choice, and that was my entertainment. I finished the book as fast as I could and visualizing myself living in the story. When all the other kids were at home living wonderful to me, I just dream and dream. In the eight grade my friends Judie and Stephanie always had real stories to tell. During school recess they would talk about how they sneak their boyfriends through the window while their mom and dad were sleeping. They talked about how they stayed out late at night and didn't even get in trouble. I was flabbergasted, so that same day, I went home and looked all around my house. I looked at every window to see which one I could sneak a boy through.

Some boy was going to come through this window and give me a real kiss, I thought to myself.

We lived in a small house. The windows were too small. I knew if I let a boy in my window, his neck would get stuck and Mama was going to wake up and beat his head with a broom, thinking he was burglar. Afterwards, she'll beat the breaks on of me if she found out I was the one letting him in the window. So, I decided I'll just stay out late. The pole lights had been on past an hour and I didn't even care. I wanted to stay out and see what I was missing. I enjoyed myself as I sat in the middle of the streets under the pole light. I talk excitedly to a couple of other kids who parents let them stayed out late on school nights and any other night.

More than usual, I skipped down the street happily, and thinking about my good story I was going to tell Judie and Stephanie during recess the next day. I knocked on my house door, and it was already open. I smile, because Mama had thought about me before she went to bed. I open the door and step my foot inside, and the lights pop on. Across my back felt like lighting had struck me. Mama had an electric cord wearing my butt out. Mama seems as if she was a monster of some sort the way she was whipping me. She scared the hell out of me.

"I see you want to do things your way!" Mama yelled every time she swung.

I didn't know what kind of parents the other kids had, but Mama wasn't having it. I went to school the next day and told my story, but what I didn't tell is how I got my butt whipped. From then on unless Mama said otherwise, I was home before the pole lights attempt to come on.

CHAPTER 10

Entering the salon to see Co-Co holding things down gave me an extra boost for today. It feels good to know I have someone who can run things responsibly if I'm not here.

"Good morning, Linda," Co-Co speaks as she put the finishing polish to Keisha hands.

Keisha is Co-Co best friend. Co-Co works on Keisha nails as long as she can when she doesn't have any clients waiting. They'll whisper and giggle all the while about their men.

I check my messages Co-Co has taken for me as I put my purse on the desk.

"Thanks, girl, for booking my appointments. Who is Tasha Wiggin?" I ask.

"She called this morning; she wants to come in today

129

for a relaxer and a semi-permanent rinse. She said you've done her hair before, and she wants you to call her to let her know whether or not she can come," Co-Co says.

I don't know right off who Tasha could be, but I'll see her when she arrives.

I notice a black Lexus pull up to the front of the shop door. *It can't be my client that quick, because it's only been eight minutes since I called her,* I thought. I continue towards the back of the shop to take my spaghetti to the refrigerator. Unexpectedly, I hear a loud noise coming from the front. I rush to see what's going on. Sidney has Co-Co on the floor beating the hell out of her. I'm speechless with my mouth open. I knew this ass whipping wasn't far, because Co-Co along with Jodie had forgotten about he is married. I search for Keisha, but all I can see is her big eyes and cell phone against her ear as she sits and stares out of her car.

"Bitch, you been in my house. I'm gonna kick yo ass!" Sidney grunt as she kicks Co-Co in her face.

"Stop, y'all have to take that somewhere else before I call the police," I scream after they have falling on top of my desk.

I don't want to press any charges on Co-Co or Sidney. The last thing I need is for my shop to be scandalized in the Yazell News Paper or on the news channel.

"Y'all need to get the hell out of my shop, tearing it up," I say.

"I'm sorry Linda, but this bitch been fucking my husband. My neighbor saw her leaving out of my house," Sidney says while standing in the middle of the floor furious.

Co-Co hasn't moved a muscle. She sprawl on the floor scared as hell in the corner by her manicurist chair, and fold up like a snail once salt has been toss on it. It's a little too late to be crying and regretful. I don't feel sorry for her.

"Sidney, I apologize for what's going on, but both of you need to get out of my shop," I say holding my shop door open.

Sidney is my client, but fighting in my shop is a no-no. I gave Co-Co an opening, but if she lives for drama, drama will always follow her. I never bring anything negative about my life to my shop, and I'll be damn if I let somebody else bring me down. I do know that Co-Co is fucking Sidney husband, but they are all grown and got to handle their problem elsewhere.

Tasha has arrives while I am cleaning up the spill acetone off my floor. It's a good thing she missed all the turmoil. Tasha attends college at the University of A&M., and I haven't seen her since last year around this time. She explains to me that she has found her another beautician who does her hair while she's at school. She works full time and goes to school full time and hardly ever come home.

Hours after the fight, Co-Co calls me to see what is up with her job. I notify her about a shop that is for lease across town. "By having your own shop will teach you business values and other things that you want know unless you get in control," I assured. Co-Co agreed that she needs her own place. She came back to the shop and got her belongings moments before I close.

Swallowing the Lump

"Good luck," I say.

Sidney calls me an hour after I got home wanting to pay for the damages, but good on her expense, Co-Co equipment is all that got damage. Sidney went on to explain to me how she sits at home day and night with her physically handicap son Tracy. Jodie works from 6:00 a.m. to 6 p.m., but hasn't been getting home till 3:00 a.m. in the past three months with his excuse being, he pulled a double.

So yesterday he said to her, "Take a break and go get a full body massage.

He'll tend to Tracy."

To Sidney that was the most romantic thing she heard in months. This morning Sidney neighbor Lorain, who visits her every morning, told her she seen the nail tech that works at Linda's leaving out of her house after staying two hours on yesterday. Sidney says she had a feeling, because Co-Co looks at her weird and is always passing by her house all day and every day.

After Sidney finish explaining to me her problem, she asks me if I will continue to be her beautician, I've been doing Sidney hair for four years. Co-Co is no longer working here, so why not.

"Yes, I'll continue to do your hair," I say promptly.

I need an extra strength Tylenol to soothe this thumping headache I got after a hard day of work and being in the mist of all the drama. Flip has finally made it home from Georgia. I missed him so much that I'm going to take him to dinner so we can talk all about his trip. When Flip is with his dad I try not to ponder them unless I really have to. Flip will call me in the morning after he wakes up and at night before he goes to bed, but during the day he's over excited with being with his dad. Being paralyze is very difficult for Patrick compared to the way he use to juggle around, but thank God progress is being made. He is able to sit up by himself and is able to live back at home.

"Ma, I had so much fun! We went to Six Flags and I rode almost everything. My dad went too, and I push him around in his wheel chair. All my cousins were there. Ma we had an awesome time!" Flip say cheerfully.

I smiled the whole time Flip talked. I even forgot about my headache. I am happy my baby had such a wonderful time. To think now of how Patrick and I acted after our breakup up just wasn't being mature parents. We both held some type of breakup grudge against one another. The grudge kept us from talking and out of sight from one another. I had to look at the picture as a whole because it was beginning to confuse Flip. After our two year grudge, I finally called Patrick on the phone and said to him, "We need to talk and get some type of understanding for Flip sake. You can pick him up on the weekends, or during the week. However, we need to work this out. He needs the both of us,"

CHAPTER 11

August 2006

School has started so I have no time to talk on the phone or go out to the club. The homework Flip has been getting for the past three weeks has been very challenging. I have to have a comprehensible mind to concentrate and help him. Middle school is nothing like elementary school. I was just learning my time tables in middle school, and now they're doing pre-algebra.

My phone is ringing, and I've been seeing this same number showing up on my I.D. for weeks. If it's a number without a name, I assume it's a bill collector and don't answer. But this time they hang up and call again.

"Hello!" I scream.

"Hello," a man voice says.

"Yeah, who do you want to speak to?" I ask with a snapping attitude.

"Is this Linda?" he asks hesitantly.

"Who is this?" I ask once more before I start to hang up.

"This is Henry, I don't know if you remember but you gave me your number," he says.

"Oh yeah, I remember," I say softly.

I almost had given up on Henry, since I haven't heard from him or seen him any more.

"I've been calling you for a minute now but I never get an answer. I'm coming up town in a couple of hours, and I was wondering if I could drop through," he explains and asks very boldly.

I vacillate, because normally I don't invite guys to my house- period—and especially around my son, unless I'm really comfortable and know them like that.

I don't guess it's nothing wrong with a friendly little visit, I wiggle my leg and say to myself.

I pray that I'm not making a mistake, but I really do want him to come over.

"Yes," I say and gave him directions and start preparing myself for the visit.

"Flip, we're going to go over your homework and get you ready for school tomorrow. I've invited a friend over to talk about old school days. Remember the time we were in the car and I waved at a guy, I told you he was an old school mate. We'll, he's stopping by this evening," I say to Flip, and I checks over his homework.

Bridgett Artis

Fried chicken breast smothered in homemade brown gravy, mash potatoes, pecan pie that I brought from the grocery store, and dinner rolls is a quick and simple dinner for Flip and me. I'm nervous and don't want to treat this as a date, so I need to stay calm for this friendly, little visit. However, I'll just keep my lounging shorts and tank top on, because I feel that if I change clothes that I'll be trying too hard and will frustrate myself.

"Ma somebody is knocking at the door," Flip walks speedily to my bedroom and say.

"Ok, I'll get it. Just continue to play your play station for a little while, and dinner will be ready," I say.

I spray my hair with holding spray before I walk down the hall and took a deep breath, then open the door. Henry eyes went directly to my pedicure feet; my brown, even-tone, baby-oiled legs; and glazed at my white shorts with the zipper in front; working up to my white tank top before his eyes connect with mine.

"Hey. How are you doing?" he asks.

"I'm good. Come on in and have a seat," I say holding the door open.

I love to talk and ask questions. Conversation is the key; whether he is lying through his teeth or is telling the truth, I can pretty much learn a lot about someone with conversation. Minutes have passed and no talking has started. I'm not use to being this quiet. I can lead, but when it comes down to a man, I like to follow. I'm waiting on him to say something, but he's just sitting on the sofa staring at me. If I begin our conversa-

139

tion, it's going to be a lot of talking and questions ask. Ok, here it comes.

"Would you like some cherry Kool-Aid?" I ask pouring me a glass.

"Kool-Aid is great," he says.

"So what do you do for a living?" I ask as I handed him his glass of Kool-Aid.

"I work for this company name Bills' and Sons Tree Service. We cut down log trees," he says.

"How long have you been working there?" I ask. "Wait, excuse me," I say focusing on Flip before he answers. "Flip!" I call.

"Ma'am," Flip says as he comes into the living room.

"It's time for you to eat so finish where you are on the game and wash your hands," I say.

"Yes, ma'am," he says.

"Henry this is my son Flip,"

"What's up lil man?" Henry speaks and shakes Flip hands before he leaves the living room to freshen up for dinner.

Henry is not making any conversation; I assume he's enjoying my lead. He just doesn't know that I'm excited with talking and asking question, and if he don't up his game, I'ma be seeing him reversing out of my driveway.

"I've been working for the company for 10 months," he says with a glaze in his eyes.

Henry eyes are following me with every angle that I move. I'm getting nervous because those are the same eyes that I saw in my dream. I feel like I'm dealing a hand of cards playing match yours with mines. *But remember, it's just a visit and don't entertain him inside of the dream,* I thought to myself.

"Who do you live with?" I ask.

"Since my divorce, I've been living with my mother," he says.

"Oh," My mouth drops. "You were married," I say and pause. I'm thinking hard and have a thousand more questions that's going to follow this question, if he doesn't start talking or leave first. "What happen that caused you to get a divorce?" I ask.

"Mama, I've been to prison," Henry say as he sit up straight on the sofa with his hands held together. "When I saw you at the restaurant, I've been thinking about you ever since, but I didn't want to come at you wrong. If you want to know the whole story, I'm willing to tell you," he says.

As soon as Henry said the word prison, I immediately got scared as hell. The words *reverse, reverse, reverse* kept repeating themselves in my brain.

Here I am sitting in here with these short-ass shorts on, and no wonder he's staring at my leg, I thought.

Just the word prison alone, in man's world, have meanings that will terrify you and make you run the other way. I don't even know this man. My son is in the back, and I always tell him right from wrong, and that trouble is easy to find but hard to get out of. And for him to pay attention to the company you keep. Now is the time I need to practice what I preach. My immediate thought is to tell Henry to get the hell out of my house and please don't call me no more or come back over here.

God what am I doing? Please help me handle this, I pray silently and quickly.

I look at him in a rage of fear thinking and still praying at the same time.

"Flip! Come on, and eat," I yell.

Flip and I are sitting at the dinner table eating. Henry is quiet. I didn't look up, I just continue eating. I drink my Kool-Aid and finally build back up the nerve to look his direction.

"Would you like something to eat?" I ask slowly.

"No, thank you. I can leave if you want me to." he says with his hand on his chin.

"No you don't have to leave," I swallow my Kool-Aid and say.

Henry sees that he has made me feel tight, and now he wants to leave. For some reason after sitting at the dinner table eating and thinking, I want to hear his story and know him more. Dinner is finish. I kiss Flip, and we both says, "Good night and say your prayer."

I wash my hands and clean the table before entering the living room.

"Do you allow smoking in your home?" he asks.

"Yes, you can smoke," I say handing him an ash tray.

"Do you smoke?" he asks.

"Yes, sometimes," I say.

"Have one?" he asks.

"No, thank you," I say and sat across from him on the other sofa.

Bridgett Artis

"I moved to Birmingham when I was twenty-one years old. On my twenty-second birthday I went to a club. I met two dudes; one was name Brad and the other one name Justin. They hipped me to a lot of things about the town, certain neighborhoods, and what area to flow in. One day we were riding and smoking weed. I was in the back seat of a two door Chevy Camaro. I was high as hell. There was this old, white man walking. Brad pulls to the sidewalk. He jumps out and put a gun to this man head. Justin got out from the passenger side and demands the man to give him all of his money. Everything was happening so fast. I tampered with the seat until I was able to let the seat up. I jumped out and said, 'Lets get the hell away from here,'

"Did y'all kill him?" I asked dreadfully.

"No, we got back in the car. Two hours later we stopped at a store to get some gas. The police pulled up and Brad took off running. The police had Justin up against the car. I walked out of the outside restroom and polices were everywhere. Justin and I went to prison,"

"What happen to Brad?" I asked.

"Brad was found six months later murdered behind an old building." After twenty-six months I got out on probation. I met this girl name, Sharkenda. We got married, and now here it is six years later we're divorce. We have a four-year-old daughter name Brittany. Sharkenda met and wanted to date this guy in the same law firm as she. For the last five years I was working doing construction with Wades Construction Company for the hospitals in North, Birmingham.

Sharkenda said that she wanted to get a divorce, because we were just too opposite."

Listening to Henry story didn't astound me a bit. I don't feel sorry for him, because Mama always said; *you make the bed you lay in, and how you make your bed determines how you sleep,* I thought to myself.

It took me a long time to figure out the sense to the saying. Now I take it as, I can make my life hard or I can make it easy. And at that time, hard meant getting my behind whipped, and easy mean if you behave you won't get a whipping. And Mama always stood by her word.

"I must be going now. I have to get up for work at 5:00 in the morning," Henry says and stands.

I walk Henry to the door with an ear full to my brain.

"Can I call you again?" Henry turns around at the door and asks.

"Sure you can call me again," I say and smile slightly as I close the door.

To be honest, for some strange reason, I like the way Henry open up and matched his cards. But this isn't a card game, I must remind myself, this is my life. A lot of things is going on and has gone on in Henry life, but I myself ain't perfect.

God, please have my back on this, because only you know, I pray.

CHAPTER 12

I roll myself over and look in the mirror that sits in the headboard of my bed. *Boy, my skin looks as radiant as ever,* I say to myself. My butterfly was at top speed last night, and the damn batteries went dead. I guess that's what I get for being greedy and working myself in an over drive.

I hear a car pull up in my drive. I reach to get my slip that hang on the pole of my bed. I put it on and walk to the door and peep through the peep hole.

"Ma, what you doing out so early this morning," I say opening the door as she walks in.

"Flip left his gym shoes yesterday, so I brought them by before he gets on the bus," she says.

"Thank you Ma. I haven't gotten Flip up yet. I'm gonna

147

drop him off at school today on my way to work," I say trying to stand in front of the ash tray that sits on the coffee table, but Mama notices it anyway.

"Who's been smoking a cigar?" Mama asks and sits on the sofa.

"I had a friend over last night. We went to school together," I explain.

"Do you like him?" Mama asks blushing.

"Ma, it's not like that. He came by and we just talked," I say.

"I don't know," Mama pause. "I haven't heard you say you had company in a long time. Beside, it's nothing wrong with giving somebody a chance. This could be yo husband," Mama says and she gets up to walk in Flip room and wakes him up. I hurry and dump the ash tray and put it up.

"Good morning, baby," I say to Flip as he walks into the bathroom.

"I'll be going now. I'll talk to y'all later," Mama says.

I had to put a rush on things, because I forgot to set my alarm clock, and if Mama had not come over, I would have overslept. Sometimes my body seems as if it is train and will wake up on time without an alarm, but this morning Mama was my alarm clock.

"Hurry Flip lets go so you want be tardy. I know I'm slow, but you and finding your hairbrush in the morning is beginning to be an every morning thing. With you trying to keep them waves in your hair is driving me crazy. Starting tonight I want you to have that hair brush on your dresser before you go to sleep, or I'm going to get you up an hour early," I say rushing and wondering, because I can't even get myself up an extra hour early.

"Yes, ma'am," Flip says and brushes his hair.

Our morning ride to school consists of us talking about school and anything else I can think of to talk about. I start every conversation off like this, did you remember, do you remember, don't forget, no talking in class, please listen to the teacher, and write you notes down, because I can't help you without your notes. Oh— make an A+, and did you put on any deodorant. It's a mouthful, but I try my best to get it all out.

"When I took you to the bus stop on last Friday, you must have been shame to give me kiss on the cheek like we do every morning?" I ask.

"Ma, it was a lot of kids out there," he mumbles.

"So, you best to believe that half if not all of the kids out their kisses their mom, dad, or grandparents before they leave home," I assures. "Ok. I love you," I say surely.

"I love you, too," he says and kisses me on my cheeks before closing the door. Sometimes I repeat the same things over and over again and Flip will say, "Ma, I remember every-thing you say."

My baby is growing up and I guess a kiss on the cheek before getting out at the bus stop may not be the thing. I know he's becoming a teenager soon and peer pressure is com-ing in all direction. Now is the time for me to take our con-versation to the next level about using your own mind.

Swallowing the Lump

★★★★★★

Entering my shop this morning, I miss Co-Co. She always knew the latest gossip. But being alone is what my mind need. I can get my mediation together, especially when I'm not busy. Since I've been working without her, I have new clients waiting for me in the parking lot and ringing my phone off the hook for appointments. It's so paradoxical that just how helping other people can have an effect on your life and career. To me, I wasn't suffering for business, but it was affecting me mentally and more like raising another child. Now Co-Co can talk about or do whatever she wants to do in her own shop. Having your own business is good, because your rules are your rules. However, too much of business sense and meditation is driving me nuts; I need some exhilaration.

Sweeping the shop floor I hear a tapping sound at the window.

"What's up, Sam? What are you doing on this end of town so early? The liquor store doesn't open until 10:00," I say.

Sam always stops by every other day. When he's not drinking, he talks with all the sense in the world. But when he's drunk the whole town knows. I can handle him when I'm here alone, because I know and he knows that he want bust a grape. He'll takes the trash out, and do whatever else it is I need him to do. Once I even tried to let him mop the floor, but he was too intoxicated. Sam drenched the entire shop and then fell in his mess. I had to put him out that day. The next

150

day he came back clear-headed. I explained to him what had happen, and he apologized as usual.

"You want me to help you?" he asks.

"Yeah, take out the trash," I say.

I know he wants a couple of dollars to get a tall can of Colt 45 until the liquor store opens. Before I give him the two dollars, I like to talk to him while his head is clear. His conversation and company is interesting and appreciative when he hasn't been drinking. After drinking his alcohol, he is totally the bravest monster in town.

"Thank you," I say.

"You got two dollars you can let me have?" he asks after placing the trash bags into the trash cans.

"Sit down, I'ma give you two dollars in a minute," I say.

"Gull, I can't sit down; I need a drink. Give me two dollars; I'll be back," he says.

I gave him the two dollars, and he went to the store and brought me a mellow yellow drink and him a beer.

"How you know I like mellow yellow?" I ask him and take a swallow.

"Gull, I know what you like. Ain't that's what you always ask for," he says and turns his beer up that is covered by a brown paper bag.

"Sam, you are not fixing to get drunk in here. You need to go," I say holding the door open.

Sam gets up and laughs. The beer made him feel good momentarily. Sam will stop at a couple more places across town and get his hustle on until he has his desire feeling for the day.

"Good morning Alexis," I speak.

Alexis invited me to her church six months ago. I visited her church and enjoyed myself. Alexis is the type that everything is all about her, and she is better. She says my church is old fashion, because all we wear is dresses or skirts instead of pants suits. We don't have drums and praise dances and so forth. I like my church, so you know I had to, I mean, I wanted to defend my church.

"It doesn't matter what you wear or how you praise God, as long as you praise him. When I came to your church, I know you say that you wear a nice pants suits and stilettos. Pants are my everyday wardrobe, so when I walk in church on Sunday mornings I love to have on a dress or a skirt. It brings out the lady in me," I say.

I found myself in a conflict with Alexis every time we talked about our churches. She was excited about her new church and I'm happy for her. However, that particular conversation was driving me in a muddy ditch. When two people are confuse in life and quote words that they hear somebody else say ain't doing nothing but hindering them selves. I had to learn that because I was doing it myself with Alexis. Now I don't even fix my mouth arguing with anyone about who's right and who is wrong. I just examine me.

"Girl, my husband didn't like my hair last week," she says.

Tell your husband to do it him damn self the next time, I thought instantly.

152

Bridgett Artis

I'm not married true enough, but women get on my
nerves when they say my husband this and my husband that.
Tell you husband to go to hell sometimes. He doesn't know
shit about your hair. He can't tell his other woman how to
wear her hair and better yet her hair looks better than yours or
just like yours. The thing is for you to have some decision for
yourself and what you like. I mean, all man may not cheat, but
you get my point. I know men need to and have to show
some type of interest to women about their hair or the women
would say, "You haven't notice my new hairdo or how my
hair look. The truth is ordinary men don't care about hair as
long as it is clean, decent, and you is happy with it; then they
are happy with it.

"You said that you liked your hair last week before I let
you out of the chair," I stated.

"Well, you know when you get married things change,"
she crosses her legs and says.

*Yo ass been married four months, you don't know shit about
marriage besides you propose to him,* I smirk and say to myself.

"You'll see, just ask any women who is married. And
they will tell you the same thing," she says.

Whoever this bitch has been talking too lied to her. And
yes, I'm sorry, but she's a bitch. She doesn't know, but her
husband is on the down low, and I'm not telling her happy ass
shit. She thinks she is more than anybody. No wonder she has
no friends and I don't have a shit load myself, but I know how
to socialize. She never gives you your credit about nothing, yet
instead she always brag on herself.

153

"You need to come over and see my new house. We live in the white people neighborhood. It's so nice, I love it," she says.

I know you do, that's why your ass can't afford to get a full hair care anymore, trying to live like the Jones, I say to myself.

"We're going to get us an S.U.V. this weekend," she says as she turns the Essence Magazine.

I'm trying my best not to explode before I'm finish with flat ironing her hair. But steam has already seeped out my ears.

"Are you ever going to get married?" she asks.

See, I told you she is a bitch. Not a bitch, but a damn bitch!

"No, I'm in no hurry. I haven't found a real man with some sense, a job, and that can screw me right," I say and roll my eyes.

"Our marriage isn't based on sex we might have sex three times a month," she says and pauses. But the only thing that I can't understand is he loves anal sex more than vaginal sex," she says.

I burst out to laughing.

"What's funny, you never had anal sex?" she asks.

"No, well," I paused. "I tried to, but it wouldn't fit. I was curious once, and my hot ass said, 'Let's try something different, I want to try something different,' I turn around and got on my hands and knees like a dog. I froze while he addressed himself surely, and waited patiently for the insertion. I felt something, and didn't know what in the hell had stuck the hole of my ass, but it didn't feel like a dick. I bucked and turn around.

I sat on my ass so swift, and said, 'I change my mind. That shit hurt,' I say to Alexis seriously with frowns in my forehead.

'You have to relax, and keep working with it. Once the penis is in it feel good,' Alexis says.

'Yeah, I hear the process, and I really believe you, but I took the pain as a sign that this ain't for me.' I need to stick to my original, magical, grip pliers, and let the rest alone. I'm curious, but some things I don't want to do and choose not to know. Sex is just like drugs. They say that if you are curious and try one drug you feel so good and after a while you'll upgrade and try another and another. Sex is the same which serves a wonderful purpose, but has to be respected and balanced. If your curiosity gets the best of you to upgrade, and after you upgrade, it feels so good that you'll try more and lots of different and curious new things. You yourself have to know the stopping point of curiosity which is having a strong mind, control it, and put the breaks on fast. Being too curious will leave you hanging and searching for more, and now, curiosity can eventually kill you," I say and walk in the restroom to get me some tissue for my nose.

"Anyway, you mean to tell me y'all are newlyweds and haven't had sex but twelve times since you been married. Shit, I guess better you than me," I lean in one hip and say.

"It's what and how you make your marriage. Tommy says that busy working people shouldn't focus their marriage around sex," Alexis explain.

You fool, I thought speechlessly for a second. "Oh," I say to kill the subject.

"I love my hair," she says looking in the mirror. "I hope Tommy likes it. If he doesn't, I'll let you know."

Alexis got to learn to use her own mind and have input in her marriage and stop listening to everybody else. After a while Tommy will be walking around pregnant, making the grocery, and buying his and her clothes with her money. Poor Alexis is going to be sitting on the sofa watching *As The World Turns.*

CHAPTER 13

Today is a day I had to take off. Flip has his second football game, and I don't want to be late. They had their first game last week, and I didn't make it until halftime. Flip scored a touchdown, and I missed it. I felt really bad, because he looked for me the whole first half of the game, and I was working. I explain to him that Mama may be late sometimes, but I'm coming—just keep your mind focus on the game.

Entering the gate, I immediately ask the assistance coach are we playing junior high or high school boys, because they are the size of elephants. Our boys are in black uniforms, and they are known as the Mighty Wildcats, but they put you more in the minds of wild lions. Our opponents are known as the Yellow Jackets dressed in yellow and black. The Mighty Wildcats knows they have something on their hands, because they can't pay any attention to the coach while he gives them their prep talk before the game. The Yellow Jackets rocks in their hurdle and screams, "Who are we? Who are we? Yellow Jackets, let's go get'em!" The Mighty Wildcats says nothing out loud; they just clap their hands together and run on the field. The first half into the second half has the game ending for half time at a close up, the Mighty Wildcats are fumbling and missing tackles which gives the Yellow Jackets a three-point lead with the score being 37 to 40. I get up swiftly to stand close to the gate as I can and yell, "Get them boys, don't be scared; they just look like a giant, that's all!"

With all the screaming and jumping around has my throat and lower back aching. The game ended with a score of 46 to 37. Both team joins together to shake hands. Unhappily, the Mighty Wildcats shakes hands in tears.

I return to the school grounds to wait for Flip and his team to arrive. While waiting, I think of cheerful things about the game to discuss to make Flip feel better.

"Y'all played a very good game tonight. You amaze me of the way you throw that football. I'm very proud of you," I say.

"If only we had a few more minutes on the clock, we would have won," Flip says with disappointment.

"You are gonna lose some and you are gonna win some, because your opponents have the same purpose that you and your team have with winning the game," I explain.

"This is our second L., already. We're going to win next

week. Coach Menard says that he is going to make some changes. Some of the boys that play defense may get switch to offense, and he said that practice makes perfect," Flip explains with good expectation for the next games to come.

The next morning I can hardly get out of the bed to wake Flip. Flip isn't a morning person. Most morning is a routine for us. I have to say something like this, "Baby, get up. You have three more days to go," It works everyday except a Monday morning. On Mondays I have to say, "Today is my off day, and I'm coming to watch you practice or I'll be home when you get out of school. I have to think of something to get the morning started in the right direction. I also explain to him the importance of school, and how you need school now and in the future. The school systems have change a lot, and so much is going on inside of schools. We pray every morning for a good and safe day. Thinking back to if I was late and miss the bus because I didn't get up on time, I had to walk two miles to get to school plus write my own excuse and sign Mama name. A lot have change from the way Mama had raise me. I remember everything and it work, because without the rod and hard punishment ain't no telling where I would be today. I'm a single parent who knows what's in the streets, and something about the world itself. Kids are blind, and if we let them roam uneducated and without proper guidance, they will find the path of the mighty, wild jungle, which has all kinds of detours and long paths that even I don't want to enter.

Swallowing the Lump

★★★★★★★

After dropping Flip off at school my cellular phone rings. I wasn't expecting a client to call me so early this Wednesday morning, because Wednesday morning is slow for me. My first few hours are plan out. I'm going to go jogging a couple of laps at the park, followed by grocery shopping and paying bills. If I don't proceed with my plans, I'll be off track for the rest of the day.

"Hello," I answer hoping it wasn't the school calling to explicate that Flip didn't meet the tardy bell, and they need me to verify why he is late.

"What's up, this is Henry," he says.

I forgot I had given Henry my house number and my cellular number. The last person I expect to be calling me this time of the morning would be him.

"I was on my fifteen minute break and was wondering if you wanted to go out for a bite to eat this evening,"

I assumed I asked Henry one too many questions since I haven't heard from him in a week and a half. Which isn't long, but I was looking for the call sooner, like a couple of days.

"Yeah, a bite to eat sounds good," I say.

"Bet, I'll call you after I get off with the exact time. I get off some days between 5:00 and 6:30 p.m.," he says.

I drove very slow contemplating on what I'm going to wear this evening. I've suddenly just forgotten about the hours between now, and 5:00 this evening.

Parking my car in a decent area in the park is a must for me. I need to see and know that I'm not the only lady exercis-

162

ing in this park. I have no aspiration to be on the missing person list. I see too many women and young girls who body was discovered close by or at a park. I'll even ask the next lady I see walking, "How many more laps are you walking?" Hell, I ain't taking no chances. I make sure someone is 15 yards in front of me and 15 yards behind me.

After jogging my mind and body is at it best. I finish making groceries. I paid my mortgage and water bill in full, and the rest I'll pay later. Leaving home with my closet in a mess leaves me with more work later on. It seems as if no matter how many clothes I have I still can't find anything to wear. *I'll just meditate in between time at the shop about my wardrobe and what I want to wear,* I thought.

I meditate a lot at work about my life and on the other hand making sure that I please my clients. Consultation helps me to understand my clients and to know what service is needed for them. My regular clients aren't hard to please at all, but sometimes they want my undivided attention. It can tend to be a little challenging for the day, but I come to the conclusion that everybody wants to be heard and spoiled at times.

The weather seems as if it has changed overnight. It's much colder inside the shop than it is on the outside. I know as soon as I turn the heater on, I'ma get too hot. I'm very cold nature and need heat as soon as the weather seems as if it is going to change.

"Where have you been all morning? I've been sitting in my car at the store running hot and waiting for you to get here," Motor Mouth says.

Swallowing the Lump

"Running hot, it's chilly outside," I say.

"Yeah, I like to have fallen asleep. I've been off work since 9:00. Look at you, you have them black tight on and switching like that, I ought to get your lil ass and squeeze you tight," he fusses.

Motor Mouth is 60 years old and still lives with his mother. They call him Motor Mouth because he talks too much. He claims I'm the only one who can cut his hair right. He thinks I don't know that he just want me to shampoo, rub, and cut his hair, because he pleasures himself. I give him excellent service, because I know how it feels when you have to pleasure yourself.

"You need full service or just a hair cut this morning?" I ask.

"I want full service, and what are you doing with your lips all red this morning?" Motor Mouth says cheesing from ear to ear.

"I knew you were coming, so I glossed them up for you," I lied, but that's what he wants to hear.

"I had a dream last night about you," he says.

"Look don't be taking your ass home dreaming about me at night because what happen in that dream in real life I do it better," I say giggling to myself and brushing the excessive hair from his neck to the floor.

At this peak, Motor Mouth is in la-la land. I'm shampooing his hair with every rotation I can think to do. Most importantly, I can't forget to stroke gently behind his ears while he shakes his legs from side to side. As a part of my job, relaxing

164

my clients relaxes me. My female clients need their temple rub and neckline massage well to relieve the week-long stress that build up from one week to the next. Motor Mouth is the only male client I shoot the jive with, because conversation is all he needs.

"Wake up and be still. I need to oil and blow your scalp dry," I say as I brush, rub and roll my hands around his head.

Motor Mouth is in bliss, but it's time for him to pay me and get the hell out until next time.

"I got some deer meat at home in the deep freezer. I'm going to bring you some today, when I come back up town," he says as he pays, tip and buy me my lunch for today.

CHAPTER 14

I don't know, but lately, I have been blessed to do all my clients and get off early while my finance still balance out the same and sometimes better. However, the case may be, God knows that I need a break. I made it home an hour early, which will give me enough time to call Mama and ask her to baby sit.

"Hello," Mama answers.

"Hello ma, it's me. How's your evening going?" I ask.

"Good, baby," she says.

"Mama, I want to go out to dinner tonight with the guy Henry I told you I went to school with."

"Go ahead baby, and do what you got to do. Flip will be all right," Mama says.

Mama must have read my mind that I wanted her to

baby sit. Though I knew Mama wouldn't mind keeping Flip, but I always ask her, because I know Flip is my son and my responsibility.

I quickly hang the phone up and run to my closet.

What can I wear that don't seem like I'm trying to hard? I ask myself.

My mind is blank for the right fit, so I start to look at the shoes that I want to wear, and then I'll match the fit. I know I don't want to be too dressy, but I sure as hell want to be sexy. My Banana sweater dress looks as if it is screaming *Wear me, wear me!* It's an all-purpose dress that drops from my shoulders, while accentuating and fitting tight on, and below my thighs. I haven't worn my dress, because it makes me looks just like a pretty-colored banana. However, only two bites, and I'm a mouthful. My silver, six-inch heel that has diamonds crossing my feet will do the evening just lovely. While taking my shower I'm gonna use my Elizabeth Taylor shower gel. I feel like Mrs. Elizabeth tonight. Forever Elizabeth and Henry, sound good to me. I'm stumbling out of the shower and almost slip my happy, wet ass on the floor. I stand up straight to take a deep breath and get a hold of myself. Suddenly, my phone rings, it's Henry, and he asks if I am ready.

"I will be in about thirty minutes," I say removing my slip off the alarm clock and checking the time.

Now, I need to get a move on. I'm going to dry myself off, and caress, with what I call, Mrs. Forever Elizabeth lotion all over my body. Beginning with my feet and working up my legs stroking between my thighs and inner but cheeks only to finish my caressing gently at the top of my neck. Putting on my Victoria's Secret 36D, black, strapless, lace bra, I notice instantly how juicy my breast sits. I pull my size 7, black, lace, thongs up my legs and make sure that it's adjust properly around my hips.

Victoria's Secret is going to be told if things between Henry and I keep going the way they are going, I thought to myself.

Now I'm fully dress, I'll put my deodorant on, because the last thing I need is a deodorant smudge. I'ma bump me a curl here and there, just so my hair can have the bounce it need in order for me to feather it together. Oh, I almost forgot to spray a little Elizabeth around my neck. My new M.A.C. lip gloss has been previously shining wondrously on my lips, so tonight M.A.C. gloss is my gloss. I have a few clients who love M.A.C. and suggested that I try it. I did, and I fell in love with it.

As soon as I'm completely dress, I hear Henry knocking at my door. I hurry to stuff some simple things I need into my silver, little hand purse. I open the door amaze to see Henry dressed in him a nice pair of brown slacks with a pair of brown Stacy Adams on. He looks even sexier in his dark, wine burgundy sweater accompanied by a collared brown and wine burgundy chemise underneath his sweater. My mouth drops open. Henry has surprise me tonight, he is stepping out hard. We instantly hug, and he kisses me on my cheek.

Henry, I hope you is forever Henry, because, baby, its own! I smile and say to myself.

"You look astounding," he says as he opens the door for

me. I scoot my lil, black ass in his Blue Ford F150 that sits on 22or24's; hell I don't know, but I am sitting high. This must be his styling ride and the Buick must be his work ride; whatever the case is, I'm in here. Before Henry enters the truck, I look up at the sun surprisingly as it changes to a beautiful orange that shines brightly through the front window shield upon my face. I slightly pinch myself to make sure I'm not dreaming.

I hope he talks this time so I can shut up and listen. If thing get too quiet, I'm going to have to ask a question or say something. My nerve just isn't good for the silent treatment. Henry reaches into the backseat of the truck. I turn around to see three large cases, but he only grabs one case and hand it to me.

"Find a C.D. to put in," he says.

Don't be trying to see where my mind is. My mind is far away that it's scaring the shit out of me, and you imaging to know. I'm going to have to loop this, because I'm versatile, anything goes. I open the case and begin to toss through very slowly. I flick on the side light by me and see Prince C.D. I love myself some Prince; he'll take me just where I want to be. This is problematic for me, because he has a C.D. of every artist that sings in this truck.

"I don't know what to choose," I say looking at him.

I dealt you the cards, and you want to throw them in and deal them yourself, is the expression I see on Henry face.

He put in N.A.S., CD. Anything that he picks sounds excellent to me. My choice would have taken me to the next level past high, and honestly I don't know if he is ready for my level.

"Do you eat Mexican?" he asks.

"No, all I eat is soul food. Collard greens, fried corn, pork chops, peas, squash, hog maws and stuff like that," I say as country as a pig.

Deep inside I'm laughing to myself, because he gave me another crazy expression which says, *is that all you eat.*

"Well, we're going to eat Mexican today. The first time is going to be an introduction, but as you keep eating it, you'll begin to like it. You know, pork isn't good for you," he says.

"Well, I like it!" I pause cutting my eyes at him. "I wash and cook the pork in a little vinegar," I say folding my arms.

Grandma use to, and Mama say that the vinegar draw the bad blood out and keep you from having high blood pressure. I believe them too, because Grandma didn't have high blood pressure, and nei- ther do Mama. I feel if I keep the tradition, neither will I. Praise the lord for that, I thought silently.

I cross my legs and stare at him while he is driving. He got nerves telling me what's not good for me to eat. Now every time I eat pork, I'm going to think about what he said. I'm kinda piss off.

"Oh, you never ate pork?" I ask.

"I use to until I learned better," he says and looks at me.

Please don't tell me what you learn. Please don't tell me what you learn, I thought to myself and look out the window.

I hope Henry isn't a control freak. I just can't stand for someone to tell me what to do and boss me around. I'm not bossy, I think, so I don't want to be bossed.

Swallowing the Lump

The little Mexican man came to the table with two menus. I don't know what the hell he gave me one for. I don't know where to start looking. I open the menu to look at the pictures that creates how the food looks when finish. Henry orders him a Corona and asks me what I will have.

"I'll have a Margarita," I say.

The chips with sauce and our drinks were back in no time.

"Have you decided on what you are going to order?" Henry asks.

"Look, I already told you, I never ate Mexican, so I'm going to have the same thing you order," I say.

The food was ready too fast for me. The food smells scrumptious, but it looks like cat food. Henry dips his fork into his food, and put it in his mouth chewing as if it's the best thing to his stomach. He's going for his second round, but instead of him putting the food in his mouth, he put it in my mouth. I buck my eyes and chew the food slowly, and then I swallow it. He caught me of guard, but as I chew the food it melt in my mouth scrumptiously. Henry takes turn feeding me and then himself. I'm really enjoying the baby treatment. I didn't have to pick up my silverware not once. After eating, I finish drinking my Margarita. I'm feeling pretty good right about now.

"So did you enjoy the food?" he asks.

"I loved it," I say.

I am so unwind at the end of dinner that getting in through the driver side of the truck I sit close to Henry as I can. I even turn the music up. We are laughing, and the conversation is so connecting that I hold his hand as he drives. I tell you we are just having ourselves a ball.

"I had a wonderful time this evening," I say to Henry as he walks me to my door.

"I had a wonderful time as well," he says.

Looking down standing on my door step I feel as if I'm going in a circular motion with the creative designs that is decorated into my steps, I realize instantly that I am smiling my ass off, so I immediately straighten my face. It's too early to get ahead of myself. Beside, I don't know if he is the one for me, I think to myself.

"Goodnight Linda," Henry says as he kisses me on my cheek.

★★★★★★

I stumble into the house kicking off shoes, my dress, and pulling my earrings off almost at the same time. My chest is burning like crazy. I rush to the refrigerator and immediately stick my finger into my box of baking soda. I lick the soda off my finger hoping it'll stop this burning that I'm feeling. The food tasted great, but if I have to burn in my chest as if I'm on fire, I don't want to taste Mexican food again. It's fifteen minutes after ten, and I need to call Mama to let her know that I'm on my way.

"Hello, Ma, I'm on my way to pick up Flip," I say.

"He can stay until morning," she says relaxingly.

Neither does Flip or myself wants to get up an extra hour early

175

in the morning, so I need to go and pick him up tonight, I thought.

"I better come on, so we can get a good start here in the morning," I say.

Mama only lives ten minutes away, and driving to Mama house on this Tuesday night seems as if I am the only car on the road. Listening to the radio I hear that a thunderstorm is in the forecast until 12a.m. Mama mustn't know about the storm, because there is unquestionably no way she would have let me came to pick up Flip. The moment I pull up in Mama yard, she turns the living room light on. Flip walks out tentative as he staggers from side to side. Mama stands at the edge of the porch holding her flashlight and waving her hands as the wind blows the bottom of her nightgown up to her thighs.

"It's a storm tonight," I yell to Mama.

"Well, y'all hurry up and get home before it come," Mama yells back holding the flashlight and placing her other hand over her sleeping bonnet to make sure her rollers are still in place.

Thank goodness my heartburn has gone away, because at one point, I was thinking, I needed to down an half a bottle of Pepto-Bismol. I turn the radio up so I could hear more about the weather. This is serious; the pole lights just flick on and off and the wind has pick up tremendously. It didn't seem like a storm was coming prior to Henry and me leaving the restaurant. Sensing a glare coming from the right of me, I look over and see Flip grinning at me.

"What's so funny?" I smile and ask.

"Grandma said it's about time you got a boyfriend, and

176

that y'all went on a date, too," he says.

"Y'all were having a little interesting conversation behind my back," I say and smile. "What else did Mama say?" I ask.

Mama, Kendrick, and Flip have themselves a good time around the wood heater chatting. I know because that's what we use to do. The fire would be so warm that we couldn't wait to get ourselves organize and sit around it and chat.

"That was everything," he says snuggling in the seat.

As I turn the key to open the door the wind has blown the front door open without me having to use my next muscle. The door slams open hitting the wall loudly which made me immediately check to see if a hole has occurred.

"Ma, can I sleep with you tonight?" Flip asks scarily.

Flip was eight years old when I start letting him sleep in his own bed. I must say that that was too long, but he's my baby. I had to eventually teach him how to sleep in his own bed without being afraid. It was hard, but it had to get done. However, I had no time for relation, so training my son took dedication and comfort. Even though he is 12 years old the memory is there, he stills ask me if he can sleep with me, or he'll sometimes say, "Ma will you lay with me until I fall asleep?"

"I will lay with you until you fall asleep only tonight," I say.

He is better now, because at the beginning, he use to wake up in the middle of the night and be standing above my head wanting to get in the bed with me. The last time he stood over my bed, he scared the shit out of me. It's a process, but now, he asks just to see will I give in, and if I say yes, he'll snug right in. To tell the truth, I'm a little afraid to sleep by myself. I sleep with the television on every night. I didn't use to be like that, and I wish my fear would go away simply because the light from the television wakes me up in the middle of the night, causing me sometimes not to rest well.

What am I afraid of, I guess ghosts. They do come out at night. One night I experience something with the television off and it scared the Hell out of me. A very important person I knew had passed away. He was my teacher in school, and I use to cut and color his hair. When I was in the ninth grade I never imagine doing my teacher hair when I got grown. Mr. Stevenson is his name. He was a regular client for five years. One Thursday morning he came to the shop for his every two-week hairdo. He was well and happy, or at least he looked like he was well, because he did his favorite dance he always does after I finish his hair, and he left. The following Saturday morning, I came to work and found out he had passed away. I was sadden and wanted to cry, but I had clients, so I performed quietly all day thinking about Coach Stevenson. A week after his death, I was at the shop alone. I looked across the street and saw his son David Jr. walking into the police station. I didn't take my eyes off of him. I watched him as he walked into the police station, and I asked the question, why. That same night, I hurried my son to bed before his bedtime, because I was drained and ready to go to bed. I turn all the house lights out and the television off in my bedroom. I turned my back towards my room door and doze off to sleep. Twenty minutes later, I hear footsteps, heavy footsteps. I sat up in bed and yelled, "Flip," and it stop. I got out my bed speedily and walk to my son room, because I thought he had got up and ran back into his room. I turn his light on, and there he lay asleep and snoring loud. Yes, he was very asleep. I walked back to my room and turn my television on.

I know I heard footsteps. I know I just heard footsteps, I say mystified to myself.

Five minutes later, I turn the television off, but still puzzled about hearing the footsteps. Instead of turning my back to the opening of my room door, I had my face facing the open door. I closed my eyes and doze to sleep, and this time it came to me without footsteps. I was lying on my back and immediately got startled, I wanted to jump up running, but he stood at the left side of me at the head of my bed. He put his hand on my shoulder and said calmly, "Be still, it's me Coach Stevenson." He grabs my right hand and places it on his hand so I could feel him.

I couldn't open my mouth or eyes so I smiled.

"I'm good, don't I look good," he said.

I look at the foot of my bed and saw him without opening my eyes. He had a red hat on with a feather on the side; a red jacket with a black, dress shirt underneath; and red pants on with a cane in his hand. He was smiling, his skin was smooth and light, and his hair was dark and curly just like he like it. I got scared, because he was really at the head of my bed with his hands on me so I wouldn't jump, but at the same time he was at the foot of my bed posing looking good. It was too real;

Swallowing the Lump

I panic after it start coming toward me. I open my eyes and it went away. I sat up straight in the center of my bed. I search under my covers for my remote control and turn the television back on. I thought for a moment that this shit can't be real. I jump out of bed running and turning on every light in the house. I quickly called my mama on the phone and told her what had happen. I knew it was late, but somebody needed to know what was going on in my life. Mama listened, but didn't really know what to say. I couldn't believe what had just happen. I didn't sleep in my bed that night, I slept with Flip. I didn't tell him the story, because I probably would have scared the shit out of him. I went to work and told a few of my elderly clients. Some say the dead don't come back and some say they will if they are trying to tell you something. At that particular moment, I didn't know whether or not I was crazy or other people don't have a clue to certain real life experiences. However, that night it happened to me. For a month, I slept on my couch with every light on in the house. I knew Mr. Stevenson didn't mean to scare me, so I prayed to God about it. I came home from work not long after my prayer and open my door, and I immediately felt a different feeling. I felt better and was able to sleep in my room again. However, I never asked why again. Although, one particular time, someone else I knew had passed away, so I began to puzzle myself and almost ask the question out loud to myself again. I completely had forgotten about the previous incident, but after feeling the presence of the previous experience fixing to happen again, I control the thought by completing blocking it out of my mind and it went away. A wondering mind is awesome, but can be very scary.

CHAPTER 15

A month has pass since Henry and I has been together, and all I can think about this morn ing is how we talk day and night, night and day. We can't seem to stop talking with one another. The more we talk, the more it seem like we were connected to one another. I'm so happy. I thought I was happy before by being in my own little world and keeping all my thoughts and ideas to myself, but talking with Henry has made a big difference in my thoughts and world. It seem like Henry have asked me 600 questions and I have ask him a 1,000 questions and still going nonstop. The conversation is great. Just the thought of having someone on the phone to talk to on a regular basis and go to dinner with once or twice a week has taken 40 pounds off my back. I'm even becoming a little Mexican woman. I never thought I would find someone who had experienced some of the same life experiences as me. We had memories from childhood that seem like we lived just next door. I always like to laugh, but laughing with Henry reminded me of when I was a child and my brother and I played the tickle game. Now that I'm grown and have bills and responsibilities up to my neck, laughing like the tickle game didn't exist anymore until I met Henry. Henry brought back all those fun memories. During our memorable phase, Henry tells me he wishes he could have met me before he left and moved to Birmingham.

"I was younger and you were, too. The timing just wasn't right," I assured.

This afternoon as Flip and I return home from church, following me in my driveway is Melody. I haven't talk to Melody in a few months. As long as I didn't hear from her, I know she has no problems and is doing well. I walk to her car and lean toward the window.

"What's going on, girl?" I speak.

"Your funny-acting ass won't answer the phone. I've been calling you half of the night, this morning and afternoon to tell you that I was coming to Yazell. I had to handle some business," she says and pauses. "Girl, I got a problem," she says and puts her car in park.

When Melody has a problem, it can be anything. I have to prepare myself for this conversation.

"Flip here is the keys; open the door, and go inside," I say.

I focus my attention back toward Melody after giving

186

Flip the keys.

"Do you have twenty dollars I can borrow? I need to buy me a pregnancy test," she says.

"Congratulations you're pregnant," I say, reaching in the car giving her a hug.

"I hope so. I've been buying a pregnancy test every week. You know Rodney and I have been living in Birmingham with my brother until our apartment becomes available," she says.

"Get the hell out of here. You've been doing the damn thing," I say and brush her on her shoulder.

"Everything with Rodney and I are fine; it's just my brother," she says and drops her head.

"What's up with your brother?" I ask.

"He was in a terrible shooting in Birmingham. He was chasing a guy that was in a stolen vehicle. The guy drove through an alley on 101 South. He jumped out of the car and went into an abandon building. My brother ran behind him and the guy started shooting and shot my brother in the neck and chest. My brother is in critical condition. The doctor said that he has came a long way and is progression good. He will be able to come home in a couple of weeks if things keep going the way they are going. He shot and killed the other guy on the spot," Melody explains miserably.

"I hope he be ok," I say in shock.

"Yeah, I hope so, too, but the doctor say that he may never be the same," she mumbles and pauses.

"Girl my thing is," she pauses and bites her nails. "I want

to have Rodney a baby so bad. I know that he already has kids, but I believe if we have us a baby our family will be complete."

"Does Rodney want to have a baby?" I ask.

"I haven't told him yet. I won't it to be a surprise. I've been to the doctor for examination and ask why I haven't got pregnant. The doctor says, since my cycle is irregular, it may take a while. He asked me have I been under any kind of stress. I told him not until my brother incident a couple of weeks ago. He gave me some pills that will make my cycle come on regularly, but they make me bleed too long interrupting the sex. He also said that I need to exercise and take some vitamins," she explains.

"Yo ass trying to do the oldest tradition women every made. Trap a man by getting a baby. I hope you know it work sometimes, and sometimes it don't. You know them kind of babies are call honest, sweet, little demon seeds," I say as we both laughs.

"No, girl, I wouldn't do that," she cut the laughs off and says.

I stand observing silently everything that Melody is telling me. Everything that Melody has ever wanted has finally come true. She has Rodney, and she should be happy. On the other hand the want for a baby has thrown her back into a depression. Logical thinking Rodney doesn't even take care of the kids he already has.

"Melody, when you start trying too hard, it's hard to get pregnant. Just exercise and don't think about it. The older women say that taking Geritol Vitamins can get you pregnant. Better yet, just pray about it. I tried to hold on to my twenty dollars and not add it to my offering. I guess it wasn't meant for me to keep," I say and give her the twenty dollars.

"Thanks girl, I owe you one," she says and pulls off.

Hell, when I got pregnant, I didn't know my body could hold a baby; I wasn't even thinking about a baby or anything else. I was just getting it on. Four months later, I felt something moving in the bottom of my stomach from side to side. Come to find out, I was four months pregnant. I thought my period was skipping months like the rest of the girls in school said their period did. From that day forward my life change. I was welcome, with lots of motherly responsibilities.

CHAPTER 16

November 2006

Since I left home this morning, my lawn looks as if somebody has dumped a truck load of leaves on it. Cutting my grass during the summer is better than raking the leaves and sacking them in the fall. I'm going to leave my car running, to go inside the house to see do I have any garbage bags to put the leaves in.

I only have two garbage bags left in the box and that's not enough. I need at least twelve bags. I'm going to run by the dollar store to buy some bags, and then go by Mama to pick up Flip. Entering the store I see Mrs. Essie. She immediately stops me to ask me, why her hair is breaking off.

"My beautician didn't know the reason why my hair is breaking off," Essie says.

Swallowing the Lump

"I really can't give you a definite answer, because I'm not you beautician. Medication can cause hair lost. If you are under any kind of stress that can be the problem, or it can be numerous of things. Whatever it is, you and your beautician should be able to figure it out," I say paying for my garbage bags and hurrying to get out of the store.

Mrs. Essie is lady is in her late 40's. She'll see me here and there and always asks me something about her hair. I always tell her the same thing. I guess she knows that I do hair, and that's all she can think of when she sees me.

Mama, Kendrick, and Flip is stacking firewood on the porch for tonight and in the morning. The weather supposes to get much colder later on tonight. Kendrick works and lives with Mama, but Mama say that he is considering joining the Air Force. Since he's is all grown up and I myself is grown, we hardly have time to hang together. He is trying to get his life on track, and I myself am trying to do the same thing. Kendrick met this lady name Whitney, and she is in the Air Force. We haven't met her yet, but Mama always talks to her on the phone. He thinks I'm dumb, but I know he's just trying to get closer to that dress tail— because living with Mama ain't any sexual contact going to be encountered in her house unless their name is Mama, or she leave and go to town, and have not a clue.

Mama doesn't care about burning firewood, cold or hot she'll have a fire going. I can't complain, because when it's a bad storm and the lights go out, I am the first one knocking at the door to spend the night.

I get out the car and begin to pick up the last few pieces of firewood. Kendrick speaks tiredly before going inside to take a bath.

"Mama, I need to borrow your rake. My rake is too little, and it will take Flip and me the entire evening to rake the yard with my rake," I say walking behind Mama house to get the rake.

"I'll bring it back soon," I say.

Mama don't like for her stuff to be borrow out for a long time, because she always has her own yard work around the house to do.

Flip looks worn out this afternoon, but he is just going to be worn out even more, because our yard at home need to be rake and finished before the evening is over.

"Mama, if we finish before it gets dark, can I go up the road and play?" Flip asks.

"It's going to be dark when we finish, plus you have a test you need to study for tomorrow," I say. "It'll be dark in an hour and a half, and we haven't gotten half of the yard finish," I say as I bend over to grab a hand full of leaves when I hear a man asks, "Y'all need some help?" I look back and before I open my mouth, Flip says, "Yeah, please come and help us."

Flip said it better than me, because I was fixing to say, "Hell, yeah." I guess that wasn't meant for me to say, "Huh."

Henry reverses his truck in the driveway. "It's a good thing I rode through before going home. You know I don't mind doing your yard work," Henry says as he gets the rake out of Flip hands and begins to rake.

195

Flip sack the leaves as Henry rake, and we were finish in no time.

"Ma, I see Adam and them playing ball; can I go play for a little while?" he asks.

"Yeah, just for a little while, because it'll be dark soon," I say.

Henry put all the bags on the back of his truck. "I'll dump these bags at the hay bend on the way home," he says.

I smiled with deep appreciation. By now, I'm tired of talking on the phone and hitting around the bush. It's time for new business. I walk to the back of the truck where Henry is standing watching him make sure that all the bags is tied up tightly.

"I'm cooking dinner for the evening. I was wondering if you weren't busy, would you like to come over to have dinner with me," I say.

"Dinner sounds good. I have to change my mom oil in her car, and after that my evening is free," he says as he opens his truck door to get in.

"Well, I'll see you around 8:30," I say standing with my hands behind my back.

As I run up the steps and open the door, I immediately start thinking about what I can cook that want take all night. Noticeably, I'm full of dirt and hay, but the first thing I need to do is call Flip inside, because it's past time for him to come home.

"You must have read my mind, because I was just fixing to call you," I say to Flip as he walks into the door.

"I'm going in my room to take me a bath. Run your bath water so you can do the same, and when you finish I want you to get your school clothes together, and take your study guides out so we can study. Now for what I have plan tonight I need to make sure I have everything in order and together before 8:30. During my bath I had time to think of my dinner. For a moment, I was thinking I was going to have to go by the grocery store before it close. And yes, everything in my town closes at 7:00 p.m.

Fried liver smothered in onion and gravy, rice and mashed potatoes just in case he has a preference, whole kernel corn, and a few sweet potatoes in the oven to bake with some home made biscuits is what my brain has put together.

★★★★★★

Flip and I had a time after he finish eating completing his studying before he fell sound asleep. I only have thirty minutes before Henry is here. Everything is in order except me. My plan is to get me some sex tonight. If I fuck myself one more night thinking of Henry, my toys are going to pack up and leave running. I have this cream-colored, thin, scrap, lounging dress that comes to my thighs with lace ruffles at the bottom that will fit my evening plans just perfect. Underwear, I don't need tonight, I'm just going to be bare and ready. I'm not putting on any shoes, because I want my freshly white tips that I design on my toes to be seen. I'm rubbing my Forever Elizabeth lotion all over my body and spraying a little behind my ear. It's something about my body and Forever Elizabeth that smells good enough for a man to eat and build a nest at the same time. My scented candles will burn from my living room to my bed room in a circular hypnotizing order.

"Hello," I speak after opening the door.

Instantly, my mind takes me far into my dreams that I'm mentally leaving this moment, so I pinch myself secretly to wake up.

"Come in," I say.

Henry is looking good and smelling good. I can't help but to look at his ass, back, and shoulders as he take off his blue, Old Navy jacket.

I'm going to have me a time tonight. I'm going to palm roll and spank that ass while he's inside of me. I hope he is ready, I thought to myself.

"You look lovely tonight," he says as he looks at me and bites his bottom lip. After I saw him bite his bottom lip, I knew we were on the same page. Every time a page is turn, that's just how much closer we are to the next chapter.

There's nothing I like better is to feed a man, and sit across from him at the dinner table, and watch him eat all his food without leaving a drop behind.

I got me a strong man and that's what I need, I think seriously to myself.

"Everything tastes so wonderful. The first time I was over and you cooked and offer me some, I wanted to say yes. It smelt so good, but I thought I had made you feel uncomfortable, and that's why I said no thanks," Henry says as he wipes his hand and mouth with a napkin.

"Well, my thing is I didn't want to judge you without getting a chance to know you," I say.

Now that we are full and sitting on the love seat, I'm really tiered of talking.

Me, tired of talking, I can't believe that myself, I thought.

I get up and turn the music on mellow. Prince is what I put in earlier so that I wouldn't have to search for the C.D., and all I would have to do is press play when the time is right. While I'm up I'm going to fix us both something to drink.

I wonder if apple juice is his favorite juice, but tonight I'm going to play, I want you to be all mines and not the Barbershop game. I want energy, lots and lots of energy, I thought giggling to myself.

I'm looking in the cabinet to see what size glass I want for our drink. The cute little glasses that sit to the far back of the cabinet waiting to be used have their chance tonight. I reached to the top of my cabinet where the dog rests and grab my paint of Hennessy. Hennessy mix with red bull on ice is the drink for tonight.

I see the glow in Henry eyes as he watches my every move. He can't keep his legs still or his mouth close. My every intension is to make him drool. Hell, I even want to hear him howl like a dog. I sit beside Henry on the sofa and listen to him continuing to talk about how he has been enjoying himself since we met, and how he wants to start things off right with us by being in a committed relationship.

Shit, I want to hear more, I say to myself as I take two more swallows of my Hennessy and place my glass on the coffee table. *Oh, how I love my Hennessy,* I say to myself as I scoot closer to Henry so I could look directly into his mouth. Henry put his hand on my chin, and kisses me. I closed my eyes and almost fell on the floor.

Henry put his glass on the coffee table to hold me with both hand and say, "I got you, mama." I put my leg across Henry body and sat in his lap and started sucking on his tongue and bottom lip as if I am a baby sucking on a bottle of milk. After getting into a deep mouth to mouth consultation, I pull away from Henry.

"Come follow me," I stand and say.

Henry holds on to my baby finger firmly. He follows behind me as I turn the kitchen light off. I blow out the scented candles up front leaving the candles lit in my bedroom. I slowly close my bedroom door and lock it. I guide Henry to the foot of my bed where I stop, and turn to look him face to face. Henry put his hands on my shoulders and began to slide my scraps off my shoulders until my dress hit the floor.

"You look so beautiful and damn your skin is so soft," Henry says.

I gently put my index figure on Henry lips. "Ssssssssh. No talking. Just slow rhythm," I whisper softly.

I'm standing still and looking him in his eyes butt-booty naked. I eased my hands up under his dark blue and white, sleeveless, v-neck sweater and pulled it off. Then I watch him eagerly through my door mirror as he palms my ass in a slow, circle motion. I unbutton his light blue shirt, and let it fell to the floor on top of his sweater. I rubbed my hands over his chest and gently to his back as I stood on my tiptoes kissing him. I stop quickly, and sat at the foot of my bed to catch my breath. I began to unfasten his belt buckle and drop his pants to the floor along with his Fruit of the Looms boxer.

I gaze at his penis for a moment to see what I'm fixing to be working with. *My goodness,* I think and look up in his face with a smile. I scoot back into the center of the bed watching as Henry put on his condom and knee-walk to me on the bed. Even though, we have talk about our sexual past and both of us has been tested HIV negative, you can never be sure unless you go get tested together. Therefore, using a condom for us is a must. Henry and I starts to kiss, but I slowly turns away to listen to my body drink and drink Henry fountain as if I have walk across a dry, dry desert for two years. Henry gently leans up to get on his feet, and he pulls me closer. I never thought of my 12-speed bicycle until now. I paddle and paddle, I lean to the left, and shook a leg, and paddle, and then I lean to the right, and shook a leg, and paddle, Hell, I even let the handle bars go and is still paddling. Fuck it, I even catwalk my bike. *Oh, what a wonderful ride. What a wonderful ride!* I think dimly as I shake my head from side to side.

Henry leans forward.

"This ain't over, I must leave my name," he says as he grips the back of my hair and whispers in my ear.

Henry rolls and shakes on every letter causing me to throw my head back, and hold on a little tighter. "Shit," I say and moan.

I can't play with Henry, I need to get serious, I thought.

Swallowing the Lump

I spanks his ass and says, "My turn. On ever letter, I'm going to open up an extra inch. If I faint after a letter, just get a wet towel and rub it across my face," I say as I lean back, shaking and whining like a shrew.

After the third letter, I began to hiccup, and out of nowhere Henry unwraps his tier, and stroke his tube with his hand and juices poured out of Henry hands and drips unpurposely onto my leg. My bike caught a flat after that ride, and the spare is six minutes away. During the process of waiting on my spare, I was force to meet up with a full-blooded, black bull dog. A battle I've been waiting on. I'm a half-breed myself. He came as if he is entering a battle he had never lost. We meet head to head. He rocks, licks, shakes and shakes, and found out that this battle is not going to be easy. We toss and turn, over and over until we both began to foam and foam out the mouth, but neither pit let go.

This pit is hard to tame, I think quickly. My mind has immediately starts to thinking of my next move. I stroke, and hold a long gag, and seconds later, I hear a mean howl. I knew it wouldn't be long before my opponent gives in. Unexpectedly, I find myself trembling and screaming like a wild hyena with her knees knocking. Though both animals are now stiff, and howling low, neither wants to be rescued.

"Flip!" I come to my senses and whisper out. "I hope we didn't wake Flip," I say.

I jumps up swiftly and put on my slip, and tip down the hall. I put my ears to the door before opening it. I couldn't hear a thing. I ease the door open to stand for a minute only to hear loud breathing. I turn on the light, and their Flip lay sleeping good as usual after a hard evening of work. I turn out the lights, and close the door. To the kitchen I go. In the middle of every party it's time to eat. Two turkey and cheese sandwiches split down the middle with plain potato-chips and a pickle spear on the side, will get this party going to the wee-wee hours in the morning.

CHAPTER 17

The alarm clock has scared the shit out of me. I can't believe it is already 5:00 in the morning; I just closed my eyes. Looking to the side of me, I see Henry brown ass as he pulls his boxer shorts up. Henry ass makes me want to have a partial remix from last night. I reach over, and pull him by his boxers. Henry smiles and sits on the edge of the bed. He gently bites me on my neck and shoulders while working his way to the center of my back. Vampire moves; I like that. I roll over on my stomach, and Henry climbs on top of me. I arch my back, so he can enter big head into my princess correctly. Henry rises up on his knees to get a better view at what lies before him. I help him with his view by spreading my butt cheeks open with my hands. With me shaking from side to side, and the view, it is all too much for Henry to handle. He bends forward holding himself in a folding position for a few seconds, and then falls by my side.

"I have to be at work by 6:30." He forces himself up and says while reaching over kissing me.

I sat up in bed, and rub my fingers through my hair.

"You don't have to get up. I'll lock the door behind me," Henry says walking out of the bathroom.

"No offense baby, but I always make sure I handle opening and locking my door," I say.

I have a client early this morning and Flip will be up for school in a little while, so the alarm timing couldn't have been better. I bent over to the edge of the bed, and pick my slip up off the floor.

"We're having my mom a big birthday dinner on Sunday. I want you to come," Henry says standing fully dress looking at me as I ease into my slip.

I grab Henry from behind to hold him as he walks toward the front door.

"So, are you coming?" he asks.

"Sure, I'm coming," I say.

Henry turns around at the door, and juices me up good with a kiss.

Having sex with Henry was a dream come true for me. If I could lie back down and rekindle my thoughts, I would, but my morning is coming full speed ahead. Cleaning my house and changing my bed sheets, I did as if I was on speed medicine or something. I am too energetic and happy. At the foot of my bed I see a piece of paper fold up in letter form. I open it and it is a letter from Henry ex-wife Sharkenda.

> *Hello Baby,*
>
> *I miss you so much. Things around here haven't been the same since you left. I'm so sorry. I made a big mistake when I said we were opposite, and wanted a divorce. I've been doing a lot of thinking, and it was me that was lost and confuse. You are my husband, a father, a provider, and you were doing your part to make sure Brittany and I was happy. I thought I wanted an office man to fit my life style, but my need conquerors my want. I haven't been getting any sleep for the past couple of months. I've tried calling you lots of time, but I didn't get an answer. Brittany and I need you. I know I said that I didn't want you in my life or Brittany life. I just messed up. I want us to renew our vows and start over. You were right, nobody is like you, and will treat me the way that you did. Please baby, forgive me, please, and come back home.*
>
> *Love is forever,*
> *Sharkenda.*

Ain't this 'bout a bitch, I say to myself.

I want to call Henry and tell him about this letter that fell out of his pocket, but instead I crumbled the letter up and threw it in the trash. I'm piss that this bitch wants Henry back. She threw her man to the wolves, and I rescued him. He's mine now, and he ain't going nowhere. I'm going to try to keep my mouth close, and do what I do and wait to see what happens. I know he loves his daughter, but his ex-wife can go to hell.

As I drop Flip off at the bus stop, my mind is not where it suppose to be as Flip reaches over to kiss my cheek.

"Love you and see you later, baby," I snap out of my thoughts and say.

I drove to work thinking that the letter might be some type of sign that I shouldn't ignore. I know that when you are quiet and don't say what's on your mind it accumulates a problem. So much is running through my mind, in just this short of a notice. Maybe I should call Henry, and tell him that this was a mistake, and I can't be in a relationship with him.

Hell, nah! That sounds like shit talk to me right now, I think heatedly.

I'm going to just have to be patient, because it may just be a late letter.

★★★★★★

"Good morning Alex," I say with a big smile as she walks into the shop. Alexis has lost so much weight since her last visit. My curiosity is getting the best of me, but I know enough already, and don't want to open the door for any new information.

"What you so cheerful about this morning?" she asks.

Bridgett Artis

Home girl sound and looks as if she's been hit and drag by the Amtrak train. Seem like Mrs. Bitch has issues this morning. She's never wanted to know about my happiness, so why now, I say to myself looking at her under eyes.

However, she's my client, and therefore I'm going to hook her ass up this morning. Maybe she'll feel better about herself, and go home, and put on some decent clothes.

"Girl, you know sometimes you just be so happy that you feel like skipping," I say and skip a skip to the shampoo bowl.

Even though the letter caught me by surprise this morning my dream came true. I just have to make it known to Alexis about how happy I'm feeling this morning.

"Linda before you begin to start on my hair I need to ask you for a small favor," she says.

"Ok, what's up," I say.

"I was wondering if you can do my hair on credit, and I'll pay you back on my next schedule appointment," she says.

"Lets walk into my office," I say. We walk into my office, and I close the door behind us. You are a good client. However, I don't do credit for anyone. The only way I will consider crediting you is, if you sign this consent form stating that you will pay me two dollars a day in addition to the bill for the service you receive today," I say.

"That's fine," she says and sign the form.

"I wish I felt like skipping this morning. I haven't skipped in years," Alexis say pitifully as I shampoo her hair.

My ears are definitely playing tricks on me this morn-

211

ing. This doesn't sound like the Alexis I know.

"Hello, Linda's Styling Salon," I answer the phone.

"Hey, Linda this is Jessie. I just wanted to call and tell you the good news. I graduated from the Fast Start Community College. I am now a Certified Nursing Assistance. I have a job in my home town at the Women Center in Jacksonville, Florida. I will be catching a flight out this weekend. Thank you for everything, Linda."

"Congratulations, Jessie. I am so happy for you," I say and hang up the phone. I smile to myself after hanging up the phone happily to know that Jessie is on the right track.

"Linda, I thought that marriage was what I needed to make me complete. But instead, I've been on a roller coaster ever since. I think I rushed into a marriage without getting to know who I was marrying. Tommy is never satisfied, especially with my appearance or what I do. If it's not my hair that he is unsatisfied with it's my cooking. I know that we are working people, but he doesn't want to touch me at night or in the morning. He constant complains about he is tired or his back hurts. Stressfully, I don't know what he is doing with his money, because he is always asking me for money. I think it's somebody else in the picture. I really don't know what the hell is going on. I wish I could have waited," she says miserably.

Being the compassionate person that I am, I feel sorry for her, because she's my client and I know by word of mouth that Tommy is gay. I know that working or nonworking people have a desire for sex more than Tommy is having with Alexis.

He is definitely getting his fulfillment else where. She needs to open her eyes and pay more attention to her instinct. Tommy is always waving his hands when he talks and he love to grin obsessively around men. Not to mention if he gets a little alcohol in his system, he really starts to talk proper, and his eyes began to gaze noticeably. I hate to get in other peoples business, but I need to tell her something.

"Girl, just hire you a private investigator, and maybe you'll find out something, but make sure you are ready to know whether the information is good or bad," I say.

If my husband or man is on the down low, I would want somebody to school me and let me know. Nah, hell nah, wait a minute, I said that wrong, you better damn tell me! Now this day and time you damn near have to look up his ass crack with a flash light and find out for yourself if he is receiving. If he is the inserter, it's kinda hard to tell I would guess that he loves anal. I have nothing against men or women who choose to live a secret sex life. I think it would be the right thing to do if you come out of the closet and stop involving innocent people without them knowing. Well, now I'm kinda thinking about myself. *If I see a man and he catches my sexual eye, am I wrong, for what I call honest premeditated sex that I had with him without him knowing or having a clue, and eventually make my dream come true? Hmm, that is something to think about,* I say to myself.

After turning heads today, my mind is beginning to settle back into reality. Alexis and everybody else that is drowning in their problems can verbally go to hell right about now. Their problem is their problem, and as much as I love to talk and want to help, my energy level is dropping fast. In order for me to be strong for them, I need to meditate and think something out for myself. My life has change right before my very own eyes. I never was dealt a hand that puzzled me. Now, I need my undivided attention. Before last night my own little world was control by my destiny. But now, my brain is awake and all it is asking for is Henry, Henry, Henry. I want more… more… more! If I don't catch myself, I'm going to be walking around like a chicken with her head cut off. Yes, that is a sight to see. Last night, I know deep down inside I lost the game, and I loved it.

This is real and not a dream. How could I have let myself slip away between a dream and reality? The scariest thing is, I remember this dream, but I woke up before I solved it. *Can I control myself and pretend this one off?* I ask myself confusingly. Shi….. I pause. I need help! I'm in love. This came too fast. What's the next step? I don't know. Can't know joker or spade beat this. I'm weak and my only strength is holding the duce of diamond sign high in the air and saying, *Shine diamond shine, and bring back me a winning sign.*

CHAPTER 18

Two Days Later

With everything I have going on today, I must keep my mind clear and focus. I hate to miss church, because listening to Rev. Calmly and hearing the Word gives me that extra motivation I need to make it through the day and week. Unfortunately, I miss church again today. Flip, All Star Game is this evening, and I am invited over to Henry Moms for her birthday dinner. We've waited all season for this game and now it's finally here.

A while back, I pray for someone and Henry came along. I believe Henry is the one or I just want him to be the one. I hope that I'm not wrong and shit blows up in my face. The thing is how will I know if I don't give someone a chance, but whatever happens I know God has my back. The letter really

217

has me thinking second thoughts. I could be wrong, but today I need to get to the bottom of this letter. The past few days I've been really dry towards Henry. Every time he calls or wants to take me out to dinner or a movie, I lie and say, "I'm tiered or sick," I hate to get in my mysterious ways without knowing the truth behind this letter.

You see, how little shit can mess up a good thing. I'm too mature for the way that I've been acting, so I need to act my age and not my size eight shoe size. Being a spoil mysterious bitch ain't going to get me anywhere far in this relationship if I don't squash it and act right.

It's a quarter to nine and Henry is calling.

"Good morning, pretty lady. I am calling to see are you feeling well today for dinner?" he asks.

"Yes, I'm feeling much better today. I must have had some type of stomach virus. Thank goodness it's gone," I lie and say.

You see how lies start when you keep things to yourself, and it becomes easy and easy to tell innocent lies.

"I'll be over to pick you and Flip up at 12:30," Henry says.

"Flip want be going with us this time; he have a game that he needs to be prepared for," I say.

I only have a couple of hours to spend with Henry and his family. I have the slightest idea of what and who I have ahead of me to meet.

I hug Flip as I drop him off over to my mom house. As Flip opens the car door he sees two dogs join together at the bottom pulling different directions.

"Look, Ma, Look at them dogs!" he says shockingly holding the rake tightly in his hand.

"Don't bother them; it's a magnet inside of them. They'll come apart in a little while," I say and grin.

When I was little I use to throw rocks at the dog when they were stuck until I grew and learn better. I wouldn't want anyone to throw rocks at me if I was joined together from getting it on. We'll just go to sleep and wait for our bodies to settle down. But, if I wake up and we are still stuck, I'm dialing **911**, because this is an emergency.

I have twenty minutes before Henry arrives at my house to pick me up. I assure Flip that I'll return soon enough to have him at the college before prep talk. The All Star Game is being held at the University of Alabama, and we are over excited.

I pull up to my house to see Henry park in my driveway. I look at the time thinking he is early. Thank goodness, I am already dress.

Henry is standing outside his truck pressing his foot against his tires.

"How long have you been waiting?" I ask as I get out of my car.

"Actually, I just pulled up a few minutes ago," Henry says.

"I'm ready. I just need to go inside for a minute to make sure I unplug the iron," I say.

"You need to be careful with leaving things plug up. You

know a house fire is easy to start," he explains.

That's something I already know, and that is the purpose for me double checking, I thought.

"I'm ready," I say as I lock my house door and double click to make sure my car doors are lock.

Henry cracks his window and he lights his cigar. The scent of his cigar smells different. I'm curious to know is it a new kind of cigar, but I just sits like a good, little lady with my mouth close and look at the road. I'm trying to wait on a good time to bring the conversation up about the letter his ex-wife wrote without sounding as if I'm threaten or insecure. Until I get this out, I don't want to talk about anything else.

"So....What's on your mind, because you've been mighty quiet lately?" Henry asks as he takes his C.D. out of the radio.

This is not a good time at all for me to tell Henry what's on my mind. My palms are beginning to sweat, and it feels as if I'm about to piss on myself. Why couldn't he have left me alone and let me continue to be in my own little world and stare out the window. I'm not bothering him. He is suppose to be driving and concentrating on the road and not on me. Shit, he's taking me too fast. I'm crazy right about now, and that's the way I want to be until I decide to be normal. It's hard for me to completely get out of my world and answer questions, because I just may snap. I'm not prepared for his question at all.

"Watch out for that deer!" I scream.

Henry drops his C.D. and put his eyes back on the road.

"Damn, I like to hit that big ass deer. I wish I had my

rifle, I would have shot his ass," Henry says.

I'm glad we didn't hit the deer, but he bucked across the road just in time. Talking about the letter was coming to the tip of my tongue, but Henry ex is nothing I want to discuss at this moment. Her ass is history, and this I'm certain of, but I feel that it's still some unfinished business that has not been address between the both of them. Therefore, I need to hear him say, she is history. Yes, some confusing shit, but I need to hear it.

The deer has quickly taken Henry mind off what he had asks me. By the time his mind begins to settle back, we're driving into his mother wire fence. Henry opens the fence. It is ten cars parked inside the fence and ten cars park outside the fence. I'm just hoping all these peoples are not inside this house. *What am I suppose to do with myself around all these peoples?* I thought. *It's a good thing that my son has a football game this afternoon, because ain't know way I will be able to sit at his mom all afternoon. Maybe I'll get use to it in the future, but for right now ain't no way.*

Henry holds my hand as he introduces me to his family and guest as we enter the gathering room. At this particular moment, I waved my hand and vanish mentally into my world. Henry must feels me drifting away so he squeezes my hand and brings me back. Everybody is staring me up and down. I hope my rainbow jacket and matching heels didn't tell my true colors. All six brothers and three sisters introduces their accompanying friend or fiancé. My first thought after shaking their hands is, if everybody has somebody new this Sunday, which one of his sisters or brothers will have someone new for next Sunday.

"Y'all come on in the kitchen," a women voice says.

Henry continues to hold my hand while leading me into the kitchen. I'm glad I'm not the only new guest in the house getting judge. One lady is so nervous she can't stop pulling her shirt down to her hip.

"Hello, Linda. I've been hearing so much about you. I'm so delighted that you were able to join us today," Mrs. Bash says as she gets up from the dinning table and gives me a hug.

As we hug, Henry let my hands go to walk up stairs. All of a sudden I'm sitting alone at the kitchen table looking around all crazy wondering where Henry has gone.

"Make yourself at home, get up and fix you a plate," Mrs. Bash says to me as she gets the pitcher of sweet tea out of the refrigerator.

I smile and politely look toward the stairs for Henry, but I can't see him anywhere. I grab a plate and fork and begin to fix my food. After pouring me a glass of sweet tea and sitting the pitcher back on the counter by the refrigerator where Mrs. Bash had left it, I notice some pictures of Henry and his family hanging on the refrigerator door. Erratically, I drop my glass of sweet tea to the floor. One of the pictures that hang on a magnetic frame is a picture of Henry kissing his ex-wife. Now, I'm really pissed. Why in the hell did he bring me over here, and he still has pictures of him and his ex-wife hanging up, especially on the damn refrigerator door. This is the last thing I need to see. I get a grip of myself to play the situation off.

"My hands were too full," I look around mysteriously and say out loud.

Henry promptly comes into the kitchen and cleans up the mess. After cleaning the mess Henry gets another glass and pours me some more tea. I stare him in his eyes and crack a smile and says, thank you. I'm really ready to explode. Within the last week I have held too much inside of me. This needs addressing now. Henry fixes him a plate and sits beside me at the dinner table to eat. I feel him eating and staring at me, he even has the nerves to feed me his food. I go ahead and eat the food as he put it in my mouth, but at the same I am thinking of my way of handling things. At my mom house, I have two big pictures with two different guys hanging in her living-room that you can see right when you walk into the door. They're just pictures I was asked to take a year ago at my cousin Bee-Bee Christmas party. I look stunning on those pictures, but didn't really know either guy. I was going to throw the pictures away until Mama said that the pictures look too good with me on them to throw them away, and she wants to keep the pictures for herself.

★★★★★★

On the drive to my mom house, I'm sitting as close to Henry as I can. Henry likes it too, because he wraps his right arm around me and pulls me closer. My plan is to take Henry inside to meet my mom and hopes that he sees my pictures hanging on the wall. Not that I'm trying to make him jealous or anything, but I want him to ask a question or say something about my pictures.

Henry and I walk onto my mama porch and I knock on the door. Mama opens the door and greets us both with a hug.

"Come on in. I'm glad to meet you, Henry," Mama smiles and says.

Mama offers us something to eat.

"I'm about to burst Mama, but put me a plate up, and I'll get it later," I say.

Henry wants a piece of pound cake so we sat for a little while until he finish.

"Where is Flip? I told him I will be back early in order for us to get to the game in time," I say and stand up to give Mama a hug good-by.

"He went down the street over to Mrs. Pearle house to buy him a blow pop. Y'all will see him if y'all just keep straight up the road and stop at the fourth brown house on the corner by the stop sign," Mama says.

Henry gives my mom another hug before leaving out of the house.

"The cake was delicious, and it's nice to meet you, Mama," Henry says.

I turn and walk to the truck smiling without looking back.

Henry opens the door and we sit quietly for a moment. He starts the truck, but didn't put it in drive.

"You look just like your mom and you even talk like

her," Henry pauses. "You also took some nice pictures that I saw hanging on the wall."

"Those pictures are so old. I took them at my cousin Bee-Bee Christmas party. I didn't like the pictures and was going to throw them away, but Mama said that they were too nice of pictures for me to throw them away, so she decided to keep them. I saw some nice pictures hanging on your mama wall and refrigerator," I say.

Henry scratches his head, and looks cogently my way. I look serious at him, but with an innocent, *come on you can tell me anything expression on my face.* To my understanding visible pictures of an ex means deep feelings still exists, and if he still have feelings for Sharkenda other than you the mother of my daughter and I wish you well for Brittany sake, his ass is history.

"Yeah, my mom has pictures of me and my family hanging all over her house. Unfortunately, it's a picture of me and Sharkenda hanging on the refrigerator. I tried to remove it, but the magnet frame that the picture is enclosed in is stuck to the refrigerator. The last thing I want to see is a picture of my ex-wife before I open the refrigerator door, Henry explains.

I scoots more towards Henry, and fold my left leg under my right leg, and rub his shoulder.

"Lately, Sharkenda has been calling me constantly, and leaving sorrowful voice messages on the answering machine. She's at the point to if she can't get me one way she'll think of another way. I told her that if I ever left, because of her wanting to get a divorce that I'm not coming back. However, what agitates me the most is that none of the messages are concerns about Brittany; it's all about nothing I want to hear. Luckily I have my own phone line, because it's unfortunate, that I had to move back home with my mom, and I defiantly don't want my mom be implicated with my divorce," Henry says.

Now that everything is going as plan my timing couldn't be perfect to talk about the letter.

"Oh, speaking of your ex, you left a letter on my bedroom floor. I thought it was something of mine so I read it, crumbled it up, and threw it into the trash," I say with a perk in my lips.

"Yeah, my mom stopped my truck before I was leaving out of her drive that night and gave me the mail. Sharkenda wants to work things out and get back together. I accepted the fact that I needed to call her so I did. I told her that I have moved on with my life and it's officially over between us," he says.

"My visitation for me to have Brittany start next month," Henry turns to me and says with a smile.

Henry reaches over to me and gives me a juicy kiss. "You my baby and you can stop all of that sneaky little pouting you've been doing the past couple of days, because you ain't going nowhere. I've even made reservation for us to go to the Smokey Mountains in Tennessee. They were book up for now, so we have to wait a day after New Years. You know what, that's even better, because I'll be off papers New Years day."

I couldn't hold back my smiled if I wanted to, I smile from ear to ear as I hug and kiss Henry. I feel much better after

226

our conversation. Now I can relax and be my happy self again.

"Would you like to come to Flip's ballgame today with us? Today is the last day," I say.

"Yes, you know I would," Henry responds.

I'm happy that I thought to bring Henry to meet my mom, because if I had to of done it any other way, I would have blown it out of proportion.

★★★★★★★

Between leaving my moms and picking up Flip we made it to the University of Alabama way early as plan. Flip spots his coach and runs to his side. The coach directs him to the field house for warm-up and to go over new plays. Looking at Flip and his teammates on the side line, again, they look mighty little compared to the Yellow Jackets. The Yellow Jackets had already beaten us at the beginning of the season. However, the Mighty Wildcats, and the Yellow Jackets won overall as the best in their league for the season. I just hope Flip doesn't get tackle by six players where everybody jumps on top of him one by one with him being at the bottom. My first responds when we get home would be, "You don't have to play anymore if you don't want to. But on the real, the last thing I want to do is make my son fear the tackles, because if he can take the hard tackles now, he'll be able to handle them in the future."

The weather is so cold, I wish I had brought Flip a long-sleeve, union shirt to go underneath his jersey. Even though he and his teammates are doing a good job warming up on

227

the sideline before the game and have forgotten about how cold it is, I am freezing.

With today being our first time inside the University of Alabama football field, the field looks amazing. I feel like we have already made it to the professional league. I am now officially, a football mom! Chunky Soup Commercial, here I come!

With the score being tied up the first half 14 to 14, I was a bit concern, because Flip couldn't get a good throwing pass in. He skillfully made both touchdowns by running the ball through the middle. The other team has caught on to what Flip is doing, and starts to rush in on him causing him to throw an interception. Now it is the end of the first half, and the Yellow Jackets' score is 21 to the Mighty Wildcats' score of 14.

Jumping around and screaming for Flip and his teammates have me all warm up, whereas to Henry, he's sitting beside me fold up in a knot blowing through his hands.

"Come with me, so we can get a cup of coffee. I never go to any football games, but watching Flip and his teammates is tripping me out on how boys their age can tackle," he says as he stands with his hands in his pockets.

Standing in the long line for coffee it seems as if everybody wants the same thing, coffee. I got out of the line to use the restroom while Henry stays in line to get our coffee. I'm happy that I have company at this game. Normally, I'm good sitting alone and cheering my son on, but today having my company, I feel a different good. Although, Henry isn't use to being at a football game no more than watching it on television, just having him freezing beside me makes me happy.

The second half has started and the Mighty Wildcats is off to a good start. No one has scored yet, but…wait a minute… #25 Dewayne from the Mighty Wildcats has recovered a fumble from the Yellow Jackets and run sixty yards, and he scores a touch down. The crowd and I go crazy, even Henry is out of his seat clapping his hands. The score is tied up 21to21. The Yellow Jackets has the ball but can't get the first down and the ball is already back in the Mighty Wildcats hand. Flip sees that his wide receiver Bobby is open forty yards down the field and throws him a scoring pass.

"Touch down!" the referee screams.

Henry and I jump out of our seats and run to the gate. I can't stop here, so I'm running to stand on the side line with my picture camera, and immediately start taking pictures. Flip pose on one knee with the football in his hand as I take pictures until all the films are out. I turn to walk back behind the fence, and who I see standing on the field with one crutch is Patrick holding a video recorder. I gave a delightful waved and smile and return back to Henry side.

Patrick has caught my attention. I couldn't help but look across at him again, because it's been a long time since I seen him standing and walking. Patrick hasn't been in Flip life much, but the time he shares is precious than not at all. I guess when the parent relationship separate, no matter how you look at it, the children are separated a little from the other parent that leaves the house as well.

Swallowing the Lump

The Mighty Wildcats won the came 28 to 21 and receive, The All Star Trophy. Flip is awarded MVP for the season. He starts running toward me with his trophy until he notice his dad and instantly run and hugs him. Flip walk and talk with his dad until it is time for us to go. As Flip runs to me, I screams and say, "We won, we won, we shot that bee-bee gun!" Henry shakes Flip hand and say, "Way to go, Flip, you and your teammates did y'all thing."

CHAPTER 19

December 2006

A full house cleaning on Monday is my routine I do on my off day. My house isn't nasty, but the trash and dust I don't see when I'm rushing or working all the time is what I find in areas I want see until I began to move furniture around. If I could afford a maid, I probably wouldn't hire one, because I'll find myself wanting to hire a cook next. I turn my radio up louder when I hear my favorite song, Lovers and Friends by Usher featuring lil Jon and Ludacris. It sounds like I hear a knock at the door as I squeeze out the mop, but it's too early in the morning for anyone to be knocking at my door. I began to see my door knob turn and Henry opens the door. Just that fast I had quickly forgotten I had given Henry a key. I turn the radio down and greet him with a kiss.

"What you doing home so early?" I ask.

"Hey, baby," Henry says and kisses me back.

He sat on the sofa with his baseball hat in his hand. He rests his elbows on his knees and began to scratch his head. Henry is silent.

"What's wrong?" I ask.

Henry didn't say a word. I couldn't read his mind, so I continue back to mopping my kitchen floor. I look over at Henry as I dip the mop and began to squeeze it out.

"I can't read your mind, so are you going to tell me what's wrong?" I say as I dip and leave the mop in the bucket with both my hands spread open and staring at him.

Henry gets up and stands in the front door looking outside. I can't stand the favor of the silent treatment, so I dry my hand with paper towel. I walk over to stand by Henry to look out the door as well. I fold my hands up and look up in the tall pine trees to see what he is looking at. I didn't see a thing, but birds, trees and the sky. However, I just stand quietly and look crazy too.

"My boss got a new contract deal in New Orleans. Since Hurricane Katrina he says that they are paying more money to get New Orleans build back up. He's going solo and leaving out by the end of the week," Henry says with disappointment.

I look at Henry and unfold my arms.

"You act like it's the end of the world since you lost your

job. There are plenty of jobs out here you can get. Southwest Paper Mill is two blocks from here and they are always in need for help. Better yet, you get you a morning paper and go to the help wanted advertisement and see what you can find," I say and walk back to the kitchen to finish my mopping.

Henry acts like he didn't hear anything I just said, because he is still standing in the door and looking lost. I'm off all day and we have the house to ourselves. The first thing on my mind is him getting some of this hot wet pussy of mines. That's all he needs is a shot of this pussy to let some of his frustration off. I finished mopping the last corner beside the refrigerator and sat the mop outside the house behind the back door to dry. I wash and dry my hands to go wrap them around Henry as he stands in the door.

"Sugar, don't worry," I say squeezing his jaw. "You'll find something, I know you will. One monkey don't stop no show. I know some important people with their own business. I'll help if you want me to," I say and rubbing my hands around the back of his head only to work my way down to caress his neck and shoulders.

"Thanks, mama. I love you so much. I needed to hear that," Henry turns around and says while giving me a kiss.

"You welcome," I say smiling and continue back to kissing him.

Henry held my face with his hands as I suck on his tongue. We are so tied up into each other that we forgot the door is open. My next door neighbor passes by and blows their horn. You know the ones that look in your door every time they pass by, even if the door is close.

Henry closes the door, and we continue to kiss and kiss. Henry slowly works he way down to kissing my neck while taking my breath away as he slides his tongue down to my nipples, and jiggling my breast with each stroke. I vaguely steps back against the arm of my love sofa. I pull my long, mammy-made, green ruffle, cleaning skirt up to my hips. I lie back easily on the arm of my sofa and spread my legs open for Henry. Henry drops his pants to address himself, and in my pussy went big head. Big head is my own special play name that I gave. Henry lifts and holds my hips with a tight, but gentle grip. I'm enjoying every second to minutes of big head and watching Henry facial expressions. However, the arm of the sofa and my back just isn't agreeing with one another, so I push back from Henry and sit up.

"Sit on the sofa," I say.

I drop my skirt to the floor and kick it out of the way. I pull my coffee table closer and sat on Henry backward folding my leg one at a time to his side. My pussy is so wet. Henry is going to need an umbrella when I'm finish. I rocks up and down and around and around real gently on big head until I found the right angle. I lean forward to put my hands on the coffee table. I began to work my hips as if I'm at the County Park riding a see-saw and merry-go-round put together.

Henry is just lying back with his eyes close while I work him into relaxation. Steaming with sweat, and the stickiness that I feel lubricating between my thighs, I easily stand to my feet with the purpose of giving my muscles a chance to relax.

"Come take a shower," I say shaking Henry as he stares in a state of shock while looking at the ceiling.

I stand in front of Henry to rest my back against his chest as the water poured onto our skin. Henry bathes me first from neck to toe, and then I switch places with him to bathe him from neck to toe.

The silent treatment is long gone. I feel one hundred percent better and Henry is smiling and more relax as well. I hope he feel like I do, because I can run a five-mile race right about now, nonstop. Henry is dressed and sitting back on the sofa. I slip back into my clothes and sits beside him.

"Have you ever thought about going back to school to get some type of trade?" I ask looking at him with my hand on his knee.

"You forgot, I been to prison," Henry says.

"And, what's that got to do with anything," I say with frowns in my forehead.

"The system is lock tight and finding the correct code isn't easy. You can't do shit with a felony on your record. My past hunts me constantly. If I could turn back the hands of time, trust me, I would. Now that I look back at my life, I missed something, and it's like I'm dying to catch it again. Baby, it's hard. I mean, I don't want a hand out or shit like that, but a nigga just want to make it," Henry says.

"What do you think you miss?" I ask softly.

Henry hesitates before he speaks. "I missed listening, understanding, and balance," Henry says as he slightly turns his head away from my direction. "I'm sorry baby for bring this to you like this, but this shit needed to have come out. Every time I think I'm on the right path, I get hit with ditches and no stop signs," he scratches his head and say.

I paused for a few seconds thinking and listen to all of the anger and excuses Henry is making. Its hard living righteously, I know. Everybody gets caught up differently in their devilment, but where there is a will, I also know that there is a way, I thought quickly.

"There is no need to be living in the past. The future is what count. The system may never change or seem right, but you can. People can give you or us a title, and we ourselves run with it and however live with it and make it become true. For instance, you are a prime example. You've been to prison and is living the life they say an ex- prisoner lives only because the system or whoever say so, said. You don't and shouldn't let that control your spirit or your life. My theory and what I say is, 'Devil, you is a lie, and leave me the Hell alone!' I steps out on faith; just pray and believe in the good Lord," I say and pause. "I know that there is something you like to do or dreamed of doing, because everybody should have a dream," I say and walk to the heater to turn it down.

"My dream got killed a long time ago, before and months after I had gotten married," he says with a pathetic, dreamless look on his face.

"Tell me, I want to know your dream," I say excitedly.

"Can we change the subject? It's forgotten about now, and I don't even want to talk about it," Henry says looking into the refrigerator for the left-over tacos he cooked last night.

"Please tell me, please. I want to hear," I say pulling on

his arm.

Henry walk back to the living room, and I walk right behind him like a baby girl that follows her daddy around the house.

"Ok... you want to know what my dream is," Henry hesitated and says.

"Music..." he pauses. "I like to rap. I always wanted to rap," Henry says standing firm looking at me.

I look at Henry and burst out to laughing. I have to sit down on the sofa after hearing that. *Out of all the things to be, he said a rapper,* I thought continuing to laugh.

Henry put his hand in his pocket and gives me a look like; I shouldn't have told you shit. I straighten up and took the grinning off of my face. "I'm sorry I didn't mean to laugh, but when you said you rap, it was just funny to me, because I never heard you rap or sing," I say.

"Anyway, that's the dream," Henry says and opens the microwave oven to check on the tacos.

"I want to hear you rap! I want to hear you rap! Please, I want to hear you," I hold him by his arm requesting excitedly.

Henry smiles a little as he fixes his tacos. "My mind is not on rapping right now, plus I like to have my instrumental C.D. playing while I rap," Henry says making an excuse.

I let go of Henrys' arm to go dig at the bottom of my C.D. stand for an old instrumental C.D. that I have had for years. I place the C.D. in the stereo and turn the base up on max.

"Here, now you can rap, please," I say smiling.

Swallowing the Lump

Henry starts to rap, and, boy, he is flowing so hard that I start to dance like we were making a video. I'm dancing and shaking my ass so, Henry couldn't help but to give me a shout out in his song. I laugh and keep on with my dancing and shaking. My dancing, shaking, and dropping it like its hot has gotten the best of me; I need a glass of water. After I stop dancing, I reach to turn the stereo off.

"Wait, I got another one I want you to hear," Henry stops me from turning the stereo off and says.

I done got something started. Henry is rapping like he can go on forever.

★★★★★★

It's Christmas Eve, and Henry is taking his daughter along with all the early gifts Santa delivered back to meet Sharkenda in Knoxville, Alabama. The drive is an extra hour outside of Birmingham which leaves me waiting and missing them already. Brittany is so cute, sweet, and precious, but if I had to spin like a ballerina one more time, I will be living in a Tylenol bottle. I'm in shape for football and ballerina is something that is going to have to grow on me.

Sharkenda has issues, Henry explains to me, and hasn't except the fact that he has moved on and their marriage is completely over. She calls Henry threaten to keep him from seeing or talking to his daughter, because of his relationship with me. Yet the next minute, she's calling him if Brittany sneezes too loud just to hold a conversation. I know Henry

240

loves his daughter and I wouldn't dare want to be the reason for him not seeing or talking to her. Therefore, I keep my distance for now and let them handle whatever it is they need to handle concerning their daughter.

The crowd is crazy this evening. Doing last minute Christmas shopping is exciting to me, but this year I can't get out of the stores fast enough. The crowd is irrational. Two ladies on the far end of the supermarket have gotten into a fist fight over the last 32-inch television that is marked 50% off. It's a blessing that the Southwest Paper Mill gave Henry a job right on the spot, because ain't nothing like a working man.

"Baby, I'm exhausted and hungry. I'm going to pull over to Apple Bees," Henry says as he drives into a parking space.

"Beep…, Beep…," Henry cellular phone lets him know he has a voice message.

Henry checks the message and put it to my ear.

"You damn bastard. Why did you let Brittany sleep between you and that bitch?! I asked her everything and she told me. She even said Linda comb her hair. You'll never see your daughter again," Sharkenda says screaming.

She hangs up and calls again, but Henry didn't answer.

For her information Brittany was scared to sleep alone. Furthermore, I wasn't going to get out of my bed and sleep in the other room for no one. Flip is on a ball sleeping alone in his bed, and I'm not going to break that. Hell, I'm still a little afraid myself. So that's why Brittany slept with us, I thought to myself.

"Now you see what I mean when I say Sharkenda is crazy," Henry says and shakes his head.

241

Swallowing the Lump

"Everything that is going on in Sharkenda life is her fault. I was there, and she didn't want what I had to offer, and now it's over. We have to get along for Brittany sake though. I don't, and never said a word to her about whom she is dating, but, just take care of my little girl. I told her ass to leave you out of this, but anyway she is crazy," Henry fusses.

Henry put his phone back into his pocket. He reaches over and apologizes and kisses me.

"She wants to come between us, but I want let that happen. I promise," he says.

To be honest, the nagging bitch is getting on my nerve. On the other hand, I'm not going to let Sharkenda lost out ass, or nothing else, get in the way of my happiness and kill my holiday sprit.

★★★★★★

My day between Christmas and New Year's Eve has me full of joy. Flip is happy and can't get enough of riding his four-wheeler. If it was left up to me, and money grew on trees, I would be still at home lying in bed resting up for the New Year's party tonight. I schedule all my appointments for first thing this morning. As a result, I'll have plenty of time to get home and enjoy the rest of my evening.

My clients are all glistening and full of sprit this morning. That makes me feel good to know that I'm not the only one happy, because I've had my share of the holiday blues. Lonely is one thing, but being lonely on the holidays can totally be the worst loneliest.

"Good morning Alexis. Have a seat and I'll be with you shortly," I speak and say.

Alexis looks cute this morning with her green-and-white-all-over workout suite, and white Nikes on.

Time is passing by quicker than I realize, but Alexis is early this morning. I'm glad, because I'm turning heads like I have a million dollar prize at the end of my work hour.

"I need full service today," Alexis says as she sits in my chair.

Alexis and I are quiet as I base her scalp. I'm enjoying myself as my mind drifts far into tonight about how much fun I'm going to have tonight and the next couple of days off work.

"Linda it's something I need to tell you," Alexis says crossing her arms.

"Hold that thought and just sit for a minute while I pull Mrs. Brooks rods apart," I say to Alexis.

Mrs. Brooks is one of my elderly clients who isn't hard to please at all. All she loves to get is a relaxing shampoo and a curly, rod set.

"Baby, I appreciate you fitting me in at such short notice. I didn't plan to get my hair done this week until my daughter told me she is having a New Year's Eve dinner at her house tonight," Mrs. Brooks say as she pays me.

"No problem. You are a good client and I always appreciate your business," I say.

Cleaning my work area, and placing my rods in the cabinet I feel heavily that Alexis has something that she needs to get off of her chest.

"I know you heard the news that is floating around about me," Alexis says.

"No, I haven't heard anything about you," I say.

"I was sleep and awaken late the other night after I heard a funny noise coming from my living room. I got up to see what was going on, because Tommy had started sleeping on the couch about a month ago. Tommy said that his back hurt more when he is in the bed. When I hazily entered the living room I caught Tommy having sex with his friend Dillard. I fainted after I saw my husband sticking his dick into another man ass," Alexis say and pauses.

"Damn, I haven't heard any new news about that," I say shocked.

Alexis didn't need a private investigator after all.

"I haven't heard any talk, but it seems as if everybody is staring at me. I thought Dillard might have told somebody and the word is out," she says.

"You are just paranoid; people are going to talk and look. That's people, but you have to be strong and not let judging words or eyes make you shame and want to hide. Ain't nobody perfect. You'll be surprise of the same people that looking and judging you of how many skeletons they have in their closet or some type of issue," I say comfortingly.

"I didn't leave my husband after what I saw. We are trying to work things out. Tommy said he is bisexual and didn't want to tell me, because he thought by marrying me would change him and cover up his denial sex life. Tommy says he loves me and that he will stop having sex with men and wants us to stay together. I don't know what to do. I join a fitness gym to help with a lot of the frustration that I have on my mind. My weight is dropping tremendously and not because of the exercise, but because of all the emotional stress I'm going through. I love Tommy and don't know what to do," she says.

"Well, I know what I want to say and how I can say it, but girl, I can't help you with this one. You and your husband are going to have to take this to Jesus. Just get on your knees and pray. Jesus will give you an answer, but you have to listen and do as He says," I say seriously as she pay me and sign her signature on the consent form stating that she has paid me.

After giving Alexis her service for today, I can't help but to wonder, what has she gotten herself into. My life to me has been full of surprising things but never as surprising as what she has discovered or seen. Shit, his ass and Dillard ass would be full of buck shots by the time I would've gotten through with them; shit, fucking in my living room.

My mom caught me by surprise as she enters the shop.

"What are you doing here?" I ask excitedly and begin to clean up the shop. "I know you ain't driving, Mama, because normally Kendrick is shuffling you around," I say with a smile.

"I got my new eyeglasses yesterday, and now I can see to drive myself. Kendrick passed his test for the military, and he will be leaving next month. Now I have to prepare and start back to driving myself around. Anyway, I brought this Black Hair Magazine from the grocery store. I want you to cut my hair like Anita Baker has her hair on this picture," Mama says and sits in my chair with the magazine spread wide in her lap.

"Mama, what's gotten into you? You never talked about getting your hair cut," I laugh and say as I wrap my shampoo cape around her neck.

"Mama is like Stella. She got to get her grove back," Mama says and crosses her leg.

Mama is tripping me out talking about getting her grove back. This preparing herself back to driving is taking her back to the Mama I remembered.

After I finish hooking Mama up like Anita Baker, she stands up and shakes her behind from side to side.

"Baby you done hook Mama up. I fixing to go home and get my fire wood together for tonight," she says putting on her red lipstick.

"What you glossing your lips for?" I ask.

"Between here and my house, I don't know who I might run into," Mama says grinning.

I smile and shake my head.

"Mama, Henry and I want to go to a New Year's party tonight. I was wondering if Flip can spend the night over to your house. Patrick will come by your house tomorrow to pick him up so he can spend a few days with him and his family," I say quickly catching her as she leaves out the shop.

"You know you don't have to ask me that. Yeah, he can stay the night," Mama says folding her magazine under her arm.

"Flip and I will be over a little later," I turn around and

say before Mama gets into her white Toyota Camry.

★★★★★★★

While Flip and I spend time over to my moms, Henry did the same with his mom before we join together in a night of celebration. I haven't met Henry cousins Teddy and Ricky since they've been home. But all Henry talks about is the big parties they have and tonight is going to be the biggest of them all. Henry knows that he is limited to what he can do, because of him being on papers. He had to remind me a couple of times that he is on papers, because I'm quick to say, let's go to the bar and have a couple of mix drinks, listen to the music, and unwind. Music and a mix drink is my favorite entertainment. I love him a lot, so I'm willing to be patient, because he'll be off papers soon.

Its 11:30 p.m., Henry and I leaves for the party in my Mustang. I have no idea where the party is being held. All I know is where we are going there is no need to be sophisticated. Henry informed me earlier that we are going to a real celebration where the crowd will be crunk and off the chain. It really doesn't matter to me, because as long as I feel sexy, I'm all right. My black, suede, Hollywood boot that I purchased from HSN and my black mini skirt by itself says the party, party, party. Not to mention of how, my low-cut, red sweeter that shows my shoulder and the top of my juicy breast screams, the New Year is yours Linda!

I look over at Henry while he drive, and I start to shake

247

my leg after a tingle came through my entire body and stop at my clitoris. Henry is too sexy. Henry is sporting hard with his dark blue, LRG jeans and his blue and white Enyce jacket, a white T-shirt and his black and blue Jordan's. I want to slide closer, but the gear is separating us. Blissfully, I reach over to hold his hand while he drives.

I feel like I'm in another world. It's New Year's Eve, I'm happy, and I have my man sitting here beside me. What else could a lady ask for? Henry pulls over to the side of the road and rushes to the passenger side and opens my door. I'm sitting in the car watching his every move and wondering what has gotten into him. He pulls me by my hand and leads me to the front of the car. Henry picks me up only to kiss and swing me around and around and says, "Happy New Year's baby!"

I was so caught up in my own thoughts that I had forgotten all about the time. Presently, we continue to kiss and kiss as Henry swings me around in his arms.

The outside party is too much for my eyes which have me terrified to get out of the car. Guns are being shot in the air and fireworks cover the sky like magic. I can handle the fireworks, but seeing a guy intoxicated standing by his car unloading a shot gun is scaring the shit out of me. Henry and I are standing outside my Mustang. I'm having a hard time. I don't want to go inside since I can see what's going on outside. "This party is here in my home town, and I've never seen or been to this place a day in my life," I say frantically.

Henry is trying to convince me that everything is going to be ok and that it's a New Year's party and people shoot their gun. That part I know, but hell, a highly intoxicated person leaning on his Chevy Capri ain't got them all right about now.

I eventually listen to Henry and calms down. Stopping at the entrance Henry tells the doorkeeper his name and we enter inside. I don't no what to call this place a club or a barn, so I will just say a building. Two ladies looking almost as fly as me greet us and lead us through the narrow hall to the back. I squeeze Henry hand a little tighter as I follow.

"What's up, dawg? You miss the count down," a tall light, brownish, nice looking man stand up and say while giving Henry some dap.

"What's up, Teddy? Man, I'm glad y'all came through," Henry says.

Henry and I sit down, and champagne is being poured from table to table. Guys are walking up to Henry as if he has won some type of championship. I finally calm completely down while looking around and enjoying the party. This party is crunker than I imagine it would be. In every direction that I look there is something going on. In the corner to my far right is a pool tournament. To the left is a card and chess game. The center stage has colorful lights flashing with exotic dancers sliding down the ceiling on a pole. My eyes are full, I have to close them for a second or two and let them rest.

Henry puts his arms around me and asks, "Are you all right?"

"Yes I'm all right," I say with sips of my champagne.

"This is my cousin Teddy. Teddy this is my lady, Linda,"

Swallowing the Lump

Henry introduces Teddy and me.

"I have one more cousin I want you to meet, named Ricky. He's in here somewhere," Henry tells me closely in my ear trying to keep from yelling over the music.

My eyes are dimly as Henry introduces me to his cousin Ricky. All I remember seeing is two ladies escorting him to a private room near the back entrance. I turn to look back to get a good look, but Henry wraps his arms around me as we walks out the door.

It's 3:30 a.m., and Henry and I leave the party as it continues to jump off full speed. From Henry, the champagne, smoke that circulated the building and just the whole excitement itself has me horny and spinning. I feel like I'm inebriated. Henry seems normal as he opens my door and fastens my seat belt.

"This girl is crazy!" Henry screams out loud as he gets into the car.

"Who is crazy?" I ask as I turn the heater up.

"Sharkenda. She called me forty-eight times and left me fifteen messages. Talking about, I'll never be happy and she'll see to it that I want. She is really tripping," Henry says.

I stumble in the house kicking my boots off and throwing my clothes in the corner of my hallway. My bed is where I need to be. Henry pulls his side of the covers back and immediately starts to kiss and rub my shoulders. I rolls over and climb on top of him laying my head on his chest while he enters inside of me. Rolling in a circular motion I keep my head on Henry chest as we just relax and enjoy what feels like paradise as our body locks together.

CHAPTER 20

January 2006

Holding my ear to the door I can't hear a mumbling sound. The knock came again and this time it is much louder than before. I swing the door open ready to curse, whoever it is knocking on my door this hard, completely out.

"Mrs. Bash. What bring you over this time of the night? Come in," I say as I tie my scraps together on my house coat.

Mrs. Bash comes in with her big, black coat unzip, a colorful scarf around her neck, and her eyes are red as fire.

Mrs. Bash begins to talk so loudly, and Henry is the only word I can understand coming out of her mouth.

"Calm down Mrs. Bash. I can't understand a word you are saying," I say as we stand in the door.

Swallowing the Lump

"Henry told me to come by here and tell you to come by the police station to see him, before they take him back to prison," she says angrily.

"What happen?" I ask putting my hands on the side of my face.

"Somebody robbed the 24-Karat Jewelry Store on 24th Street. Henry and his cousins Ricky and Teddy meet the description a witness called in and described. I asked the officer to explain to me how they know that this information is accurate. The officer says the witness was driving pass the jewelry store when the robber took place. The witness also told the police that the car had an out-of-town license plate." Mrs. Bash says and pauses to catch her breath as I stare at her speechless. "Teddy car met the description, so the police pull them over and search them. The money that the police collected from the three of them didn't match the amount that was stolen nor was the jewelry found. The police still took them all in for custody. Ricky and Teddy was later release, because of the lack of enough evidence. The damn basters kept Henry though, because of his previous record and say that he definitely matches the witness description," Mrs. Bash says as her eyes glaze with redness.

I'm in shock and my mind is blank. Just within a blink of an eye the word prison has taken me into a deep hole so cold, wet, and dark that I never dreamed of going.

"Hurry up before they take him. I've been there an hour already, and I have a headache. I'm going home to lie down," she says and leaves weakly.

"What in the hell have I gotten myself into," I ask myself out loud. Mrs. Bash has delivered this bad news to me and talking about she has a headache. Shit, now I have fifty headaches running around in circles with birds chasing them and singing songs that I can't understand. Mrs. Bash gave me the impression that she is tired and has had enough of this prison shit.

I'm standing still like a mummy after Mrs. Bash has left, and the birds has stop singing, only to hear the word prison repeating itself over and over again in my brain. I begin to put my white Reebok on in slow motion. I open my closet and grab the first thing I lay my eyes on, which is my white, Max Studio, velour jump suit. I jump into my Mustang and pull off without giving it time to warm up. I'm nervous, and I just don't know what to do or say.

I pull up beside the police car that is park in front of the station. I get out the car and take a deep breath before entering the station. My hands are shaking so bad until I have to hold them together before they shakes off and leave me. A tall, big police walk towards me as I enter the door.

"Can I help you?" he asks.

I look in his face and then at his name tag that reads, Sergeant Maze.

"Can I help you?" he asks again.

"Yes, I'm here to see Henry Bash," I flinch and say.

"Who are you?" he asks.

"Excuse me?" I say.

"Are you related to Henry?" he asks strictly.

Swallowing the Lump

I pause and say nothing, because at this particular moment, I don't know.

Who am I? I ask myself standing weakly.

I wanted to say fiancé, but our relationship isn't on that chapter, so I say, "A friend, I'm a special friend of Henry."

"Right this way down the hall to your right," Sergeant Maze says as he leads the way.

"You only have five minutes," he says pulling up his pants and walks to a desk on the other end of the hall.

I walk slowly into the room looking straight ahead for Henry, but he's not in sight.

"Hey," Henry says softly.

I stop and pause after hearing Henry voice.

I look to the right of me, and there Henry stands with one hand and leg chained to an iron, steel bench that is nailed to the floor. Tears filled my eyes and flows down my cheeks and drips on the collar of my jacket. I just can't believe what I am seeing. Henry hold out his hand that isn't chained to bench for me to come closer to him.

"I'm sorry. I never meant to hurt you. Come and let me hold you," he says.

I wash my face with the back of my arms trying to sniff back the tears. I ran to Henry and we hug each other very tightly.

"I didn't do anything, I promise. But with me being on papers there's a process that I have to go through. I hope they give me a chance to defend myself then everything will be ok," Henry says in my ear as we hug each other even tighter.

"I want it to go away. Make it go away," I pout.

"Time is up," Sergeant Maze says standing in the door.

Henry kisses me on my forehead and promises me that he will make everything go away.

Foreseeable, I know Henry is only trying to comfort me the best he can, but to be honest, he has no clue to how his situation is going to end up. My feelings are so unorganized right now and I don't know what to do with myself. I don't want to go inside the house without Henry. Knowing he has to stay at the jail tonight, I just don't know if I'll be able to sleep.

I lie across my bed in tears. I keep a lot of my personal feelings and thoughts to myself, but I know that holding painful things inside of you can cause serious illness. *Who I can trust,* I thought.

"Lord, please give me strength and wisdom to understand what is going on and why this happen to me. I just don't understand. In the name of Jesus I pray, Amen," I pray.

After praying, I call my mom to tell her what has happen. I hate for Mama to worry about me, but I know I can trust her.

"Hello," Mama answers the phone.

It's 11:00 p.m. and I know Mama is wrapped tightly under her covers. I take a deep breath.

"Ma," I pause to clear my throat.

"Huh, what's wrong?" Mama asks fuzzily.

"I know it's late, but I want to tell you something," I say and pause. "Henry got arrested tonight, and he may go to prison," I say sniffing.

"What happen?" Mama asks.

I explain to Mama everything that happened. Mama listens quietly as I talk.

"Well," Mama pauses. "Everything is going to be all right. You just go to sleep and get you some rest," Mama says in a comforting voice.

Mama has never been a person to judge anyone. She just stays positive and makes the best out of any situation, and that's one of the things that I love about my Mama.

I did as Mama said and got under my side of the covers and left Henry side well together. I grab my bear and shake my leg until I fell sound asleep.

CHAPTER 21

Tuesday Evening

Walking and exercising helps me to stay fo
cus and to keep an open mind. But lately,
I've been walking this park and it feels like
the streets are crumbling up behind me. Three weeks has passed
and Henry is still locked up. I continue to go on with my
everyday life, but things aren't the same without Henry. Henry
promises me he would write since the collect calls are expen-
sive. Everyday I check my mail hoping to receive a letter from
Henry, but I receive nothing.

Standing in front of my mailbox, I turn and open it slowly
praying for a letter. Inside my mail box are a light bill, phone
bill, and a long white envelope that's address to Linda Lax
from Henry Bash. I quickly place the bills underneath the

261

letter. I rip the letter open trying not to tear the part where Henry name and the address is, so I'll know where to send my letter when I write him back.

> *Dear Linda,*
>
> *I miss and love you so much. I been feeling down, but remembering the smile on your face is what gives me strength and hope, so continue to keep your pretty smile. I apologize for leaving you alone out there, and I promise that I'm going to make everything better. My hearing is Thursday, and hopefully I'll hear some good news. I'll keep you inform. My visitation starts this Sunday at 10:00 a.m. Hope to see you.*
>
> *Love,*
>
> *Henry*

I sit back into the car and reread the letter again. My fingers and legs are cross for Henry to have a successful hearing. I'm trying not to worry and let so much of my life revolve around Henry and this prison shit, but it's hard for me to pretend to be strong. Fortunately, no one knows but me and God what I'm going through. The hardest thing for me to do is to explain to my son what is going on with me concerning Henry. Nonetheless, I did explain, and Flip likes and think Henry is a cool person, but don't ever want to in up in his situation.

Bridgett Artis

★★★★★★

The day for visiting Henry, I'm so excited, but at the same time a nervous wreck. Besides hearing the good news he has to tell me about his hearing, I can't wait to get a juicy kiss and a hug.

Driving and hour and a half, I finally find a prison that is fully surrounded by sixteen-inch, barbed wire. I take another look at the directions that I've received from information, and this seems to be the right prison. I'm shaking and I need to pee, but I'm going to hold it until visiting time is over. There isn't any way I'm going to let any of my time to see Henry pass by. Showing my identification, and getting check is finally over and I'm on my way to jump into Henry arms. Entering the visiting room and hearing the doors closing extremely loud behind me, I almost cried and pissed on myself. I see five stools and four of the stools are already taken by an elderly man and three ladies. I sit at the far end booth that has a square window and a phone hanging to the right. My eyes are beginning to fill with tears, because I extremely hate being here, and I need a hug.

As soon as I see Henry walks in through a steel door on the other side, we spots each other instantly and all you can see are our white teeth sparkling from smiling so hard. Henry is in handcuff and has on a black and white uniform that makes him looks just like a real criminal. He picks up his phone and points with his fingers for me to pick up the phone beside me.

"So how have you been?" he asks.

"I've been good," I lie.

"That's wonderful, I'm glad to hear that," he says.

I don't want to talk about anything else. I want to know about the hearing and how things are looking for him, so I ask, "How did your hearing go?"

Henry hesitate longer that usual and says, "My hearing was here at the prison. When I walk into the room and saw three black men laughing, my sprit immediately fell. They were laughing and talking nonstop. They even ignored for several minutes the fact that I was even in the room. Finally, I was taken in consideration, so I explain my heart out. Sergeant Maze and the other Parole Officer didn't say a word, only my Parole Officer did the talking. Without any hesitation, my Parole Officer signed for me to go back to prison. Even though, I've been out for seven years and never violated or gave him any problem, his decision shocked the shit out of me. Especially, when I know I didn't do anything. I feel the decision was made before I walk into the room." Henry pauses.

I stare away from Henry, so he couldn't see the disappointment on my face.

"My case still has to go before the parole board in Montgomery, Alabama, before a decision is final. I just hope they give me a fair trial, so I can defend myself in court," Henry explains desperately.

The doors are open loudly as a sign that the fifteen minute visit is up. Words can't explain how I'm feeling right now. However, I look sadly at Henry and say; "Everything is going to work out," knowing that I have no idea of how the law about probation or any other criminal offense works.

Bridgett Artis

My immediate thought after walking out of the rest room and now sitting in my car is I can't deal with this. So much of my energy is being focus on Henry that I can't think straight. I sit in my car momentarily and watch a lady as she walks to her car after visiting her husband. The lady seems as if she use to have a high, yellow complexion and have a nice, curvy figure. Since she is doing time with her husband, her color is fading dark and her body is lose and weak from being lonely, and all the worrying she has been doing through their process. I can't do myself like that, even though I love Henry, but I also love myself.

Sitting at home with my elbows resting on my kitchen table I contemplate on how I'm going to write and explain to Henry that I can't support him mentally or physically. My hand shakes with every word that I write, but writing these words just doesn't fit my description of what I really want to say. I crumble the paper over and over again searching for the words that is shady to my mind.

Dear Henry,

Life without you just doesn't feel the same. I never thought I would find love this way, but I did. Sometimes I question God wanting to know are you really the one for me. He always say, just be patient, my child, and you will see. One side of my mind says, I shouldn't be in love with a man who hasn't found his start, but the other side of me says, his start has already started. Sounds scary when I think about

265

Swallowing the Lump

it, but all I must be is patient, and I'll see.
  Love,
  Linda

The intention of my mind was to write a letter and seal it up with an ending and no signs of a beginning. Unpredictably, after a bright light shined through the blinds of my window, my heart took over and began to write. My mind and my heart are pulling left to right, back and forth, as if they are at war with one another. My mind says, pretend and run fast as you can, because you know you always win when you run and pretend. But my heart says stand still and learn how to win without running.

★★★★★★★

Unfortunately, as time progress, the letters came, I didn't respond. Visitation day came, I didn't show up. My phone constantly rings. I am tired of having phone sex and I'm piss, because my sex toy doesn't feel the same anymore, so I just don't answer. I thought by me not talking to Henry and trying to move forward with my life I would feel better, but the truth is, I feel awful. Henry is a part of my life now, and I love him too much to turn my back on him. There must be something I can do. I open the phone book and go straight to the yellow pages to search for the local Parole Officer in the area. Searching through the phone book I see Charles W. Hitch.

"I know him," I say out loud to myself.

Charles is the man that came by my house last year and said that he is running for election for the Board of Education in my district. Charles said that he has new changes and issues that he wants to address and need my vote in the upcoming election. I smiled and shook his hand, because I knew we could use a good change. Nevertheless, I voted for him, but it's sad to say, I haven't seen a sign of a change yet. Anyway, I'll go to his office and talk to him, and see is there anything he can do or is there any information he can give me that will help Henry.

Slipping on my long, black skirt, pink sweater, and black boots keeps me warm from all the gusty wind that is blowing outside. I jump into my ride and fill my gas tank up so I won't have to make any stops for the next thirty minutes. Charles is the only hope I got. I'm nervous, but Charles seemed like a nice, black man the day he knock on my door. *I hope Charles help me,* I thought to myself.

"Hello, my name is Linda Lax. I would like to see Charles W. Hitch," I say to the secretary.

"Do you have an appointment to see him?" she asks.

"No, ma'am," I say nervously, brushing my hand against my leg.

"Just have a seat and I'll check to see if he's taking walk-ins at this time," the secretary says and picks up the phone to page his office.

"Linda, you can go ahead back, and it's the first office to your left," she says.

I hold my hands together as I walk to his office. My mind

instantly goes blank, but I quickly remember my purpose for coming so I straighten my walk and recollect my thoughts.

"How can I help you?" Charles says as he relaxes and sits back in his chair.

"Hello. My name is Linda Lax," I say and shake his hand.

Charles sat up straight to shake my hand.

"You may not remember me, but you came by my house when you were running for election for the Board of Education, and I'm very delighted that you won the election." Charles didn't respond or crack a smile, so I begin to feel out of place.

"The reason I'm here is for Henry Bash." I begin to explain how I think Henry is a nice person, and that I was hoping if it's something he can do to help him get out of prison.

"There is nothing I can do. It's out of my hands. The decision has been made and Henry folder is close shut in the file cabinet. Henry is going to have to do his twenty years," Charles says with a smirk on his face as he rests his elbows on his desk and twiddled his pen.

Hearing those words come out of Charles mouth my entire soul completely left me and fell hard to the floor. I instantly drop my head, and I can't look Charles in his face.

"Thank you," I say struggling to pick my soul up and leave his office with my head still down.

The rushing fluid that is gathering in my brain only to flow uncontrollable through my eyes is way too much for this broad-open daylight. I try to control the fluid from flowing down my face, and it gathers in my esophagus making a lump the size of an apple stop my breathing. I have no choice, but to quickly swallow, and after swallowing the lump, I burst out loudly into tears. I drive myself with and unclearly mind as far as I can, so I can't see any signs of Charles's office. I pull to the side of the narrow highway and put my car in park. I place my head in between my hands on my stern wheel and continue to let my tears run down my face. After moments of crying I hold my head up. I begin to think about how I made Charles W. Hitch feel the day he left my house. I knew for a fact he left with hope and joy, so I wipe my tears dry and start to drive home. On my way home I start to pray, "God, I'm so sorry for doing things my way, and now I don't know what to do. This is too much for me to understand. In the name of Jesus I pray. Amen."

Within a blink of an eye a voice came to me.

"This is not your battle, leave it alone, get yourself together, and I'll take care of Henry," God says.

Out of all the whippings my Grandma Mae Bell had given me, and my mama gave me, no whipping hurt as much as this. Those whippings were just examples, so I'll know when the real one comes. It's a good thing I know what a whipping is, because back then you didn't have to tell me the same thing twice, and your sure is hell don't have to tell now.

CHAPTER 22

Seven Months Later

Having my physical and knowing that I'm healthy after all the stress and pain I once endured, my life is at a new beginning. I never would have imagine that in order for me to see myself as a whole, I would have to experience someone else lifestyle to evaluate my own lifestyle. Nonetheless, I still miss Henry, and think about him constantly, but being obedient is a must for me. Every now and then, I send Henry a thinking of you card. I feel like that's what friends are for.

I've been on my third client head for an hour straight sewing her curly weave in and my nose is itching like crazy. The old saying is, "When your nose itches somebody wants to see you." Even though I haven't talk to Melody in 10 months,

273

especially since my process, as I check the I.D box, I never expect it to be her calling the shop.

"Hello, Linda Styling Salon," I answer.

"What's up, girl?" Melody screams in my ear. I haven't talk to you in so long I barely recognize your voice. I just wanted to let you that know I had twins, a girl and a boy. Rodney and I finally got married," she says with joy.

"Hold on a minute," I say.

"Mrs. Louise, I need to step in the back for a few minutes and I'll be right back," I say to my client.

I quickly rush to the backroom in the shop.

"Yeah, I'm back, I had to come to the back to talk." I pause. "Girl that's wonderful you been on the move. I am so happy for the both of y'all," I say smiling.

"Yeah, after I got pregnant, we talked about our future together, and one thing lead to another. Girl, you just got to do what you got to do," she says.

"You are a mess," I say and grin.

"Ha, ha, ha," Melody laughs hard.

"Give them twins much kisses for me," I say shaking my head from side to side happily and considering that Melody is going to be Melody.

"How is your brother Melvin?" I ask.

"He is doing better, but the shot to his neck damage a nerve in his neck, which causes him to hold his head one-sided. He is going to counseling about the shooting incident, and about what happen between him and his baby mama. He said that he needed to talk about the incident hoping that the counseling will help him understands a lot about himself and the real purpose of his job to him," Melody explains deeply.

"That's good," I say.

"It's about time the police found out and arrest the guys who robbed the 24 Karat Jewelry store on your end of the town," Melody says popping a piece of gum in my ear.

Instantly, I scream loud with joy forgetting about my client up front. "What, what you say?" I ask lowering my voice.

"The guys who robbed the jewelry store down there in Yazell were arrested. I was sitting in the living room with the twins watching the Birmingham News. It was two guys in handcuffs after selling the jewelry to an under cover police agent. They reported that a female call in months ago when the robbery took place and gave false information that link them to someone else. No information has been reported about who the female is that gave the false information," Melody says.

I jump around rushing with excitement, and take a quick peep up front at my client to make sure that she is alright, and see her touching her hair.

"I'm so happy for you; I have to get back to my client now and thanks for calling me!" I say excitedly and hang up.

Melody always said, "I owe you one." She paid me back in full today. I look up deeply to my ceiling and hold my right hand up and say, "Thank you, thank you."

Swallowing the Lump

★★★★★★

A couple of months have passed since Melody told me the news about the arrest of the real robbers. But it's not for me to worry about the rest, I remind myself.

I'm sitting on the edge of my bed brushing my hair for church. My phone rings with an unknown call, and the last thing I need is a distraction about a credit card bill that I created when I was 18. I ignore the ring, and I leave the room to make sure Flip isn't slowing around getting dressed. Seeing that he has beaten me getting dress lets me know that I'm the slow poke this morning. Walking back to my bedroom I hear my answering machine beeping away. I reach on my dresser to get my Forever Elizabeth perfume. After spraying my wrist, I walk to my nightstand and press the button to check my message. Rubbing my wrist across my neck I freeze after hearing Henry voice.

"Hello, pretty lady. I wanted to call to say, hello and I miss you a lot. For the last few months, I've been working on my music, and I got a record deal with the South Side Records Company. I was wondering if you weren't too busy, would you like to go to the Smokey Mountains with me this weekend?"

"Henry! Henry!" I scream and press the repeat button.

★★★★★★

Henry voice message surprise me and distracted me the whole

276

while Rev. Calmly preached. The few hours I spent in service today had me feeling like I've been in church longer than usual. If I was ask right about now what service was about, I couldn't respond. Flip slept the last hour of the service, so I know his mind may be as blank as mine.

Waking Flip so we can get out of the car, I realize that I forgot to stop by Mama to eat dinner. Boiling chicken breast and rice want take me long to whip up, so I'm not to focus on missing Mama's dinner today. My first thought is to check my I.D. to see if the number where Henry called me from is known. Unfortunately, it's unknown. However, now I'm puzzled, because I can't call Henry back.

"Flip, get off the sofa," I say strictly. "Go take off your suit, and hang it in the closet. Wash your face with a cold towel, and clean your room. Dinner will be ready soon," I say walking towards my bedroom. "Oh," I say turning around, "I haven't checked your homework for tomorrow, so bring your homework and lay it on the kitchen table," I say.

Washing my chicken breast and pulling the unwarranted fat off, my mind is flashing on and off thinking about Henry. I wonder how he is doing and what he's thinking. I'm well eager to see him, but most of all I miss his company and our tender conversations. Remembering the conversations we once had of how he considered his dream dead makes me smile, and think as I rinse my chicken off, how a dream never dies, and that it's only up to you to make it real, and stay alive.

CHAPTER 23

After the court hearing of Tony Strove and Carl Lengiton who allegedly robbed the 24-Karat Jewelry Store in Yazell, Alabama, they were both taking into custody. The two guys pleaded guilty and were charged with both first-degree robbery and distributing stolen property to an undercover agent.

Sharkenda catches the last ending of the Birmingham morning news before she leaves her three-bedrooms and one-bath two-story home that was custom design by her and Henry before she leaves for work.

"No one knows about me being the unknown witness that called from Birmingham to the Yazell, Alabama police station with false information of who the suspect is," Sharkenda talks out loud. "Watching the 34/20 late night news on New

Year's night and seeing that a robbery had taken place in Yazell, Alabama, was perfect timing for me to frame Henry."

I hate his ass for the way that he is treating me. I'm his wife. I took him in when no one else trust him or wanted to be bothered with his ass. I made him the man he is. If it wasn't for me buying him the clothes on his back and signing for the little things that he do have, he wouldn't have anything. He'll miss and need me when he goes back to prison.

"My idea worked, and Henry is back in prison where he needs to be until he misses me. I know that I am a lawyer, and pulling a few good strings, I can have him out in no time. Unpredictably, since the real robbers have been captured, Henry may get release, but I'm hoping they hold him for other reasons. He'll need me soon like he always does, real soon, real soon," Sharkenda says locking her door shut.

So much has been going on with Sharkenda lately, that it is almost impossible for her to think straight and silent, so thinking out aloud calms her.

"My life is collapsing especially since my divorce, and being a single mom is hard and something I can't do. Brittany is in good hands by living with my stepmother and dad, until I get my life back on track with me and my husband the way it needs to be and is going to be," Sharkenda says as she enters her new Ford Expedition truck that she purchase as a gift to herself after her divorce.

"My life may be on the line, but there isn't any way in hell that I'm going to let Henry and that bitch lives happy ever after!" Sharkenda says angrily.

"Bomb, bomb," Sharkenda blows her horn at a car that needs to get into another lane in order to keep from missing his turn. I'll hit your ass," Sharkenda snarl inconsiderately.

"Do I have any messages?" Sharkenda ask Robin who is the skinny secretary with long blond weave that hangs curly down to her shoulders after catching her powdering her nose.

"No, Sharkenda, there aren't calls for you this morning," Robin say as she puts her makeup kit back into her drawer. "Danny says that he's in court all day today, and he left this key for you," Robin says.

Danny turned out to be only interested in late night visits with Sharkenda, and the long road for a relationship with him and Sharkenda never exist in his eyes.

"I need to get myself together," Sharkenda mumbles as she shut her office door behind her. *Stupid of me to think Danny would make a better man than my husband. His looks, career, and charm had me blinded. The time we spent together I felt like I was the one who was trying to make something out of nothing.* Sharkenda pauses and shakes her head from side to side.

Danny really shocked me when he arrived at the annual, all-white party that the firm gives every year during the Labor Day weekend. When he arrived with the winner of the Birmingham AKA First Top Model, my stomach immediately reminded me of my regretful mistake. I ran to the restroom and vomit all the devil eggs and wine up until my system felt completely empty, Sharkenda thinks pathetically while staring at her key that Danny had return.

Sharkenda place the key in her desk drawer. Glancing at the phone, she quickly picks it up, and began to call Henry sister Beatrice seeking for information. Getting information from Beatrice is like taking candy from a baby and sticking it back in their mouth when you are finish teasing them. Henry told me at the beginning of our relationship that his sister Beatrice and Sharkenda are like best friends. They constantly stay in touch with one another. Henry once said that he thinks his sister Beatrice lets Sharkenda know a little too much about her business and their other sibling business also.

"Hello," Beatrice answers.

"Hello, my sister in-law, how have you been?" Sharkenda asks excitedly.

"Great, I've been doing great," Beatrice says.

"You were on my mind, so I decided to call you. I think about you and the family a lot," Sharkenda says captivatingly.

"How is my favorite niece doing, and when are you all coming to visit us?" Beatrice asks invitingly.

"Soon I would like to come as soon as possible, but my work here at the firm has me working long hours even on my off days I'm working. Brittany has been missing her father so much until I hate to look at the sad expression on her face. You know she reminds me so much of Henry. I miss him a lot, too, myself," Sharkenda say convincingly.

Beatrice listens with great forgiveness.

"Beatrice, I know that I made a terrible mistake when I left your brother. We all make foolish mistakes, but his heart is solid as a rock towards me. I wish he would forgive me and come back home," Sharkenda whine pitifully.

Sharkenda sorry plea is only a trick to lure the information she needs about Henry and his personal life.

"Henry has been release from prison, and is doing well for himself. His dream has finally come true," Beatrice says happily.

"What dream?" Sharkenda asks wildly.

"You know the one he always talked about. When he was a little boy all he ever did was walk around the house beating on buckets, and singing with a stick in his hand. He is a rapper now," Beatrice says.

"What are you talking about? Henry can't rap, I never heard him rap. I remember once, he woke me up in the middle of the night, and wanted me to listen to some silly rhyme. I yelled at him that I'm asleep, get out of my ear, and stop sounding and acting foolish!" Sharkenda says in disbelief.

"Girl, yes, yes, Henry is on his way to stardom. He called Mama and explained it a lot more to her, but I know that he said, "He wants to get himself together mentally and physically so he can be the best father to Brittany he can be."

Sharkenda is completely quiet. "This can't be happening," she muttered.

"Did you say something?" Beatrice asks.

"No, I am just walking to the window in my office. Traffic is really heavy today," Sharkenda say trying to calm herself as she begins to boil over on the inside.

"I'm so proud of my brother," Beatrice says with joy. "I'll tell Mother to tell him that you call. She talks to him more than any of us, so I know that he will get the message," Beatrice says.

Swallowing the Lump

"No, no, you don't have to tell him that I call. Frankly, I just wanted to talk to you and say hello, that's all," Sharkenda stops and hesitate. "Sister, my secretary has walked in, so I have to go. I'll give Brittany a huge hug for you," Sharkenda says clicking the phone off with her finger.

Sharkenda water has boiled over steaming hot. She thought of the quickest lie to get off the phone before Beatrice hears the anger in her voice.

"That motherfucker, how dare he neglect me and Brittany and leave us hanging without a string," Sharkenda say as she slams the phone on the hook.

Sharkenda sits at her desk to calm all the negative emotions that she is feeling and thinking. Unfortunately, the thought of Henry and Linda being together is her greatest fear and concern.

"I can't stand the bitch, and I don't even know her. I hate her, I hate her," Sharkenda screams uncontrollable out loud. "My husband would have came back home if it hadn't been for her. Henry loves me and Brittany, and this I know for sure. The bitch Linda has taking a spot in his heart, and this I feel and know, but the bitch needs to get out of the picture now and forever," Sharkenda assures herself by knocking her cup of writing utensils off of her desk and onto the floor.

"Is everything ok in here?" Robin asks after storming into the office.

"Yes, everything is fine, I just almost trip trying to sit in my chair," Sharkenda explain calmly as she bends slowly helping Robin pick up the utensils.

286

Bridgett Artis

I'm very afraid that I will lose my job if Sharkenda finds out about me and Danny steamy night that we had last night here in her office. Although I know that she'll never find out about me and Danny, because neither of us is crazy to tell on ourselves and lose our job, but we have to be more careful.

"Danny isn't you afraid that we may get caught," Robin asks Danny.

Danny was enjoying every minute of the sex that he and I had on top of Sharkenda desk. The continuous steamy nights that we shared having sex on her desk has me worried that we may have left the wrap of the condom behind.

"You open, and put this condom on my dick like a professional," Danny said. "Baby I am a professional; they don't call me Mrs. Blond head Secretary for nothing. Keeping Trojans and working a desk is my best job. I want you to Relax and enjoy how fast I assume this position, and work totally focus on your keyboard, because when I finish with you, you will be giving that key back to who it belong to, Robin thinks about her night with Danny last night worriedly.

"Is there anything else you need me to do?" Robin asks standing with her hands held together looking at the desk and on the floor suspiciously.

"I need to go for a coffee break. My client will arrive after lunch, and I should be back in enough time. However, I need some coffee," Sharkenda says breathing slowly as she stands to her feet. "Would you like anything while I'm out?" she asks.

"No, thanks, I'm fine," Robin says.

287

Swallowing the Lump

"Damn she is awfully jumpy this morning," Sharkenda mumbles after Robin closes the door.

Sharkenda decides to walk to the coffee shop across the street from the firm about a half a block away next to Movie Gallery. The atmosphere is pleasant, and the music is mind relaxing.

"Good morning," the waitress speaks. "Would you like a menu?" she asks.

"No, I'm just having coffee, a large cup of decaffeinated with no cream please," Sharkenda requests.

Sipping her coffee and gazing out of the window at the passing traffic Sharkenda is relaxed and listening to the music. She didn't notice that her cup of coffee is getting low until the red-head waitress appears in her face asking, "More coffee, ma'am?"

"Yes, please," Sharkenda says.

"We are now going to give you the all new and most requested single, "If I Choose You," from the one and only Henry Bash. Henry album, *Intermediate*, is in stores December 20, 2007," the radio DJ announces.

Sharkenda can't believe what she hears from the radio. She sits in disbelief as she listens to Henry entire song. Sharkenda burst into regretful tears as she immediately leaves the money for the coffee, and the remaining change as a tip for the waitress.

Walking in heels with blurry eyes, Sharkenda has come to the conclusion that the bitch Linda must go, and that she has no time to waste. *Time is running out, because my idea to take Henry away so that he will miss me didn't work, so now my new idea has to succeed.*

CHAPTER 24

Friday Evening

Waiting for the moment to see Henry again has me feeling like a child waiting on Santa Clause. Ten months has been long enough, and I'm ready to play catch up. Tonight, Henry and I will be on our way to the Smokey Mountains. Flip will be well taken care of with Mama for the weekend, so Henry has my undivided attention. Every evening this week and late nights Henry and I have been glued to the telephone. He is thrill of his accomplishments and his new album that making his new video was like snapping his fingers, and everything fell in place. I must say that I am a bit anxious to see the pictures, and talk about his stay in Mamie, Florida, since I've never visit Mamie. However, I know that watching his video and seeing all the pictures will take me there.

I think that I'm over-packing, because playing dress up and tease with the lingerie and heels that I'm bringing, has taken up an entire luggage bags by itself. However, I'll keep all the lingerie, and just carry fewer clothes. Finishing my packing and jumping into the shower was an exciting blast for me. Henry assured me that we'll be leaving at 8:00p.m., and I'm already ready at 6:00 p.m.

I must be excited, because I never gotten pack and dress two hours early on no circumstances.

"Hello," I answer after barely hearing the phone ring.

"Hey, sweetie, how is my lovely lady doing?" Henry asks.

"I couldn't be better. I'm all pack and waiting for you," I say smiling.

"I just made it into town. I miss you like crazy, Linda, but before I come for you, I promise my mama that I'll swing through, and give her a lot love."

★★★★★★

As time and days progress throughout the week, Sharkenda knew that she and Brittany must take a trip to the country as soon as possible. Traveling to Yazell, Alabama, has always been a drive that she hates to take. However, seeing Henry family is the closest way of getting next to Henry, and to gather information on his relationship with Linda.

"Surprise," Sharkenda screams as Beatrice opens the door and sees her and Brittany with their Kool-Aid smile.

292

"Hello, I'm so thrilled to see y'all here," Beatrice says as she hug and squeeze Brittany tight.

"I decided to come this weekend, and surprise you and the family," Sharkenda says as her eyes focus from every corner of the room before having a seat on the sofa.

"If I had of known that you were coming for the weekend, I would have had time to get the family over for a family gathering," Beatrice says.

Sharkenda sits quietly as Brittany takes over the conversation.

"Where is my daddy? I want to see my daddy," Brittany whines.

"It's a good thing that you and your mama came down this weekend, because mama said that Henry is supposes to be home any time today. He's leaving out tonight for a special trip, but he should be here soon," Beatrice explains. "Have you heard his new single? It's has been all over the radio as the most requested song," Beatrice says tapping Sharkenda on her knee as she sit next to her on the sofa.

"Yes, I've heard it," Sharkenda says stupidly.

"Honey, why are sounding so dry? Henry is singing that song to you, and I know no matter what's going on, Henry still loves you and Brittany," Beatrice assumes. Ain't that right, my little precious niece?" Beatrice says comfortingly as she reaches over and put Brittany on her lap.

Sharkenda smiles with gratitude, because Beatrice is on her side, and still has belief with her and Henry reuniting.

"I tell y'all what; I'm going to put on some clothes to

take you and Brittany over to visit Mama. Mama will be happy that y'all are here."

★★★★★★★

With Beatrice playing the middle game, which she feels that she is a professional in, has not a doubt in her mind that she is doing anything crooked. She feels that Sharkenda and Henry should remarry and start over again. I know personally when a relationship is over, it is over.

Henry, on the other hand, has no idea who is ahead of him to meet at his mama house. He drives in fast pace in his new, black, 07 Infiniti trying to visit his mom and make it back over to Linda in enough time for them to be on their lovely way. Henry loves Linda, and believes that she is the one. Asking the big question to Linda is building more and more on the tip of his tongue. His only concern is will she be able to handle him traveling on the road a lot.

While Henry focuses on driving and listens to his C.D. for any mistakes that he can hear that no one else can hear has him in a deep concentration. Forthcoming, his mom has more company than she can handle. Brittany visit is always welcome, but Sharkenda made a messy bed with Mrs. Bash a long time ago. Sharkenda didn't want Henry to visit his mom for a long time after they were married. Sharkenda feels that since her and Henry was married, his family including his mom should come last, under all circumstances. Shortly after Sharkenda and Henry were married, Mrs. Bash was hospitalized after having a light stroke. Sharkenda didn't allow Henry to use the car to go to Yazell and visit his mom. Mrs. Bash reminded Henry time and time that there is something about Sharkenda that she just can't put her hands on, but insists that he be careful. Mrs. Bash suspicious became true when Sharkenda put Henry out of the house after he arrived home from working a twelve hour shift. Henry clothes were packed and box completely. Clueless to know that he had to leave with her plans of having Danny to move in.

Answering the door has Mrs. Bash happy as she can be to see her son Henry.

"Surprise," Beatrice says standing in the door holding Brittany hand with Sharkenda standing besides her barely hiding the fake expression on her face.

Mrs. Bash catches herself quickly from looking disappointed towards Sharkenda, and hugs Brittany tight as they all went into the dining room. Mrs. Bash talks to Brittany and hug her over and over again with great pleasure of seeing and holding her grandchild.

"Your daddy is on his way any minute now," Mrs. Bash says as she rubs her hand over Brittany, lengthy pony tails.

Sharkenda is speechless the whole while she sits until politely Mrs. Bash serves lemonade and cake. Sharkenda sees the picture that she and Henry had taken on their wedding day hanging on the refrigerator door and immediately says, "Mama, you still have our wedding picture hanging up, Henry and I was so happy."

Mrs. Bash turns and looks at the picture easily and then

looks back at Sharkenda and says kindly, "Life brings on many changes; some for the good and some for the bad."

The thumping of music quickly catches everyone attention, especially Brittany. She leaves Mrs. Bash arms and run to the door screaming, "Daddy, Daddy," as she opens the door.

Henry is happy, surprise, amaze, and shock all together when Brittany runs to the car and jumps completely into his arms. Henry holds Brittany in the air, and swings her around as he watches the glow on her face.

"Daddy wanted to surprise his baby with lots of goodies," he kiss her cheek and say, "How has my little girl been doing?" Henry asks.

"Good, Daddy, I miss you," Brittany says.

"I miss you, too. We have so much catching up to do, and I promise Daddy is going to make it all up to you," Henry assures as they walks up the steps.

Henry greets his mom with a one-arm hug with Brittany in his other arm. He hugs Beatrice looking puzzle to what's going on. Looking Sharkenda direction Henry politely speaks, and focuses back towards his mom and Brittany.

"Ma, I'm glad that you are happy. Seeing the smile on your face lights my heart more than you can imagine," Henry says.

Henry didn't go toward the dining room with everyone else. He and Brittany walk upstairs to the guest room to get his road map. Henry places the map in his pocket, so he wouldn't forget it later. Bamboozled from the surprise of Sharkenda, Henry feels uncomfortable for the first time in his mom house and immediately is ready to leave.

"Ma, can I talk to you alone for a moment," Henry says.

"Sure, son," Mrs. Bash says as she leaves the dining room, and walks into her living room.

"Mama, Linda and I are on our way out of town. We'll be back in a couple of days," Henry says as he raises Brittany up on his hip and kisses her cheek.

"Daddy will be back soon, and we'll have our own little vacation," Henry comforts Brittany.

"I love you, and be careful, son," Mrs. Bash says cheerfully. "I want you to know that I'm proud of you," she says and gives him a hug.

Henry and his Mom walk back into the dining room, and he hugs his sister and kisses Brittany with great promises for their one on one time. Henry tries to keep his distance from Sharkenda, and only wants to talk about things that concerns Brittany. Even though Sharkenda sits quietly with a sorrowful look on her face, Henry pays her no attention for conversation and leave.

Walking towards his car Henry is immediately stops with a slight pulling to his shirt.

"Henry, I know you saw me in there. Why are you acting all tough like I don't even exist?" Sharkenda pause by putting her hands on her hip. "I know I made a terrible mistake. Why can't you forgive me?" she begs.

"Sharkenda, I have been through this over and over again with you. Sharkenda, our divorce is final. When I return from my trip, Brittany and I are going to Disney World, so until then, we have nothing else to talk about," Henry confirms roughly.

Sharkenda is lost for words with disappointment and places both of her hands over her mouth. Tears fill her eyes as she watches Henry pull off speedily. Beatrice hurries outside to comfort Sharkenda as they walks slowly to Beatrice car to let Sharkenda sit down.

"I'm going inside to get Brittany, and we are going back to my house," Beatrice says.

Beatrice walks toward the house and up the steps angry at her brother for treating Sharkenda the way he did. Beatrice feels that Henry should at least talk and hear what Sharkenda has to say. "The vow was for better or worst, or until death do us part, and neither was going by the vows," she thought.

"Brittany is spending the night with me," Mrs. Bash says as she and Brittany enjoys more lemonade and cake.

Beatrice comforts Sharkenda, or at least thinks that she is comforting her, by talking about Henry relationship with Linda. Beatrice assures her that Henry is only going through a phase in his life, and that men go through uncertain phases.

"Beatrice, I left my husband when he needed me the most for another man. I don't think Henry will ever forgive me for that. I think he is in love with someone else," Sharkenda says cunningly, sniffing back her tears.

"The relationship Henry has with Linda is not like you and his relationship. Y'all have a special bond together that will never be broken no matter how many trips Henry and Linda takes," Beatrice assures.

"I know he didn't leave my daughter side to take that bitch Linda on a trip. I just know he didn't," Sharkenda say in rage.

"Calm down. In a couple of day's he'll be back for Brittany, so just calm down and take a deep breath," Beatrice pats her on her shoulders and say.

"I need a cigarette," Sharkenda says as she gets out the car. "Where is the nearest convenient store?" Sharkenda asks.

"Two blocks from here. It's the largest one by the traffic light," Beatrice says.

Sharkenda needs time to let everything that is going on with her sink in. So for her trip to Yazell has been disappointing, but now, something must be done.

★★★★★★

I can hear Henry a half a mile away bumping to his music. I get up and double check myself in the mirror, and rush to the door.

"Hey, honey," I say greeting Henry with a juicy kiss.

"I miss you, baby!" Henry says as he lifts me off the floor and into his arms.

Henry puts me down and immediately grabs my luggage, and we leave right away. The feeling I get when I'm with Henry has me on cloud nine. As we leave the gas pump, Henry begins talking about everything he has been doing with his music career. He pauses as reaches into his side compartment and hands me pictures of him and his crew working in

Swallowing the Lump

Mamie. Listening to Henry, and seeing the pictures, it seems like Henry has been having himself a wing-dang-do. Henry is talking nonstop, and if I'm not mistaken, he even tells me that he is ready to settle down and raise a family. I want to say, *back it up, you are talking too fast, because I heard something, but isn't quiet sure that's what you said.* However, the phrase was said I didn't say a thing for him to repeat himself, I just listen and listen. The fact is I'm already on cloud nine, and if he said what I think he just said, I'm going to melt like chocolate ice cream.

An hour and a half up interstate 20/59 Henry holds my hand. His palm is sweating so that it feels like my hand has sink into a large, hot, wet glove. Henry looks me in my eyes for a flash two seconds, and tell me that he love me, and that choosing me to be the one is the best thing he ever done.

I smile speechless as Henry holds my hand as we listen to his hit single, "If I Choose You."

Suddenly, out of nowhere, the wind that was created by another vehicle rushes by fiercely.

"Damn, honey, this truck is about to run us off the road!" I scream rising up to see what is going on after feeling the car wobble to the side of the interstate.

"It must be some drunken motherfucker," Henry says trying to get a good look at the vehicle, and wanting to see the license plate.

"Are you all right?" he asks sitting up, and placing his hands firmly on the stern wheel.

"That looks like the same truck that was park in front of

the convenient store I saw when I walk inside to pay for the gas," Henry says uncertain.

"I don't know who the hell they were, but they scared the shit out of me!" I say turning the music down.

Henry seems to be a little shaken up, but is trying to be cool and calm for my sake. I'm completely off of my cloud nine when I immediately see a light from a far that is headed our direction.

"Oh, my God!" I scream! "It's that same truck, baby, and it turn around. It's coming straight for us!"

The crashing of both vehicles head on is what you see in a movie and not in Linda life. Dimly vanishing away Linda hears Henry weakly voice, but is out before understanding.

★★★★★★★

"Mama, Mama, wake up," is all Linda hears as she weakly *awakes and* see a little boy and other people by her side.

Linda looks around slowly, but is simple in mind and has no idea to where she is at.

"Mama, it's me, Flip, don't you remember?" Flip say repeatedly holding Linda hand.

Linda stares at the little boy without any response. Flip reaches into his pocket and holds a picture of him and Linda close to her eyes. She tilts her head slowly toward him and slightly smiles. Shortly the doctor who has been taking care of Linda since her accident comes in the room and say, "Mrs. Linda, I'm Dr. Groove. You have been in a coma for a week.

You were in a terrible accident involving two others." Dr. Grove held his folder up close making sure that his information is the same as stated. "The female that cause the accident died on the spot. The man Henry you were riding with is on the seventh floor in ICU. The bleeding to his brain won't stop and any answers to will he survive is too soon to give."

Looking and listening without a blink to her eyes at the doctor talk, Linda doesn't understand anything, because her mind want let her comprehend. Dr. Groove turns to Mrs. Lax, Claret, Kendrick and Flip and say, "I know she may not have understand anything I was saying, but as her doctor I have to let her be aware of what is going on. It's going to take time for her to remember who you are, and some things and people she may not remember at all, so be patient and progress will come."

EPILOGUE

All Linda wanted was the right man that was meant for her. The path Linda took was excit ing, but hell-a-for-bumpy, with no warnings of the deep, cold, slippery and muddy hole that sits in the middle of the path. After slipping deep into the hole and bruising her soul, she knows that the only way to heal and live she must make a move, and fast. She manages to gather her strength and hold her head up. She sees the opening of the hole once a light has shined through showing her the sign of the way out and to survival. She skips happily away from the hole until she was suddenly stopped by a strong force. The force told her that she needed to turn around and go back, because she has forgotten something. Linda stayed still panicking for moments and wondering what she could have forgotten. Going forward

305

is all she wanted to do, but a voice says, you must go back. Slowly returning back to the deep hole, Linda searched puzzled as she stood far away, so that she wouldn't slip back inside. She looked across the street after a red apple fell to the ground. She walked over and got the apple and there she saw a dirty old sign with a hole at the top of it. Linda holds the sign up, and blew the dirt off, and it read with a pointing arrow, "Warning Deep Hole." She looked up at the tree and saw that it had a big nail stuck in it. She hangs the sign up, and continue happily back to skipping.

Linda learned a valuable lesson—where there is a will there is a way, and with that mindset not one can take her down. Henry on the other hand is slowly progressing, but is making millions as her recover. It's ironic that if a celebrity dies, has drama, or come close to dying their fame will grow stronger and stronger. However, when it's all said and done, Henry dream has came true. Growth is powerful and is extremely beautiful to the wise eye that can see growth, and understand the process of growth which will cause major enduring attraction with the bad boy turn good.

Henry relationship with Linda is positive, and is alive with him, but Linda memory with Henry hasn't been found.

www.ingramcontent.com/pod-product-compliance
Lightning Source LLC
Chambersburg PA
CBHW080859020726
47502CB00008B/2287